TO PROMISE

THE MCNALLYS

LAURA SCOTT

READSCAPE PUBLISHING, LLC

1

Flying to McNally Bay had been a massive mistake.

Brianna Murphy leaned against the white pillar of the gazebo overlooking Lake Michigan and watched the waves rippling across the surface with the breeze. The summer sun had begun its slow descent over the western horizon, and while the warmth was nice, hotter than Ireland ever experienced, she missed the green lush landscape of her home.

Why had she been so foolish? She'd never chased a man before, and she wasn't sure why she'd done so now. Despite sharing a couple of heated kisses beneath the starry Irish sky, she'd soon realized, especially after Jazz's wedding, that Jake McNally wasn't interested in a long-term relationship.

And she didn't do flings, especially with handsome American men.

So what if he'd invested in her father's farm, bringing them from the edges of bankruptcy into the best year they've had in a decade? She didn't owe Jake anything. After all, he'd made loads of quid over and above his initial investment and would for the next several years.

The fact that he hadn't asked her to accompany him to Jemma's wedding had stung. Thinking it was the pressure of the wedding itself, she'd decided to surprise him with a post-wedding visit. Not only was it a way for them to spend additional time together without impacting his visa, but she'd hoped that being with Jake and his family would make him realize what he'd be missing when he left Ireland for good.

But the exact opposite had occurred. With each touristy outing they'd taken together, Jake had become more and more distant. To the point she barely recognized the man she deeply cared about.

Was this the real Jake McNally, then? If so, the man she'd fallen for was nothing more than a figment of her imagination.

Time for her to head home and put Jake McNally out of her life, and her heart, for good.

"Bree, can I get you something to drink?" Jemma asked, joining her in the gazebo.

"No, done more than enough for me, you have." Bree smiled and hoped her sadness wasn't too obvious.

"You helped me cook breakfast earlier, so offering lemonade isn't too much." Jemma's keen gaze seemed to pick up on her morose mood. "Have a seat, I'll join you for a bit."

Bree didn't want to impose on Jake's youngest sisters who co-managed the McNally B&B more than she had already. Especially when Jake had been annoyed at her unexpected arrival. The past couple of days had passed with nothing but painful politeness between them.

It was about to drive her mad.

"Here you go." Jemma returned several minutes later

carrying two ice-cold glasses of lemonade. She handed one to Bree and then pulled the two deck chairs over.

"Thanks a mil." Bree sat more so to make Jemma happy than anything. She owed Jemma, especially after how she'd arrived without an invite the day after her wedding.

She couldn't bear to leave the same way. Jemma and Jazz deserved better from her.

"You can't let Jake's stubbornness get to you."

Bree winced. She did not want to talk to Jemma about Jake. "He has a right to his feelings, I suppose. And I shouldn't have dropped in without ringing him first."

"Bree, you are always welcome here in McNally Bay." Jemma took a sip of her lemonade. "Jake's been on his own for a long time, moving from one place to the next. I think he really enjoyed his time in Ireland."

Maybe, but she knew he'd spent far more time in England, due to the limitations on his visa, than he had in Ireland. In Ireland, visitors could only stay for 90 days total within 180 days, so Jake had made the most of learning about horse racing while he was in England. After that, it hadn't taken that long to get her father's farm running in the black. Jake helped her father buy the two-year-old thoroughbred colt they'd named Dark Rogue, then convinced Seamus Murphy to enter Rogue in a race taking place in Berkshire, England. The unknown colt had come from behind to win a decent purse in two of the races that day, and several others in the weeks that had followed. After being established in England, they'd returned to Ireland where Dark Rogue had won more races. Jake had returned to England to discuss the colt's success. Several investors had expressed interest in having their colt sire the next generation of Rogue offspring. The stud fees they were willing to pay were staggering.

The Murphy Equestrian Farm was profitable at last and would be for a long time, thanks to Jake.

If only he hadn't been so charming.

She cleared her throat. "I've come to realize Jake prefers to be on the move, and a mere woman isn't about to hold him back."

Jemma sighed. "We were so excited when he brought you to Jazz's wedding."

Her face felt frozen, as if it might crack. "Me, too," she finally admitted. "But I sensed a subtle change in our relationship after we returned to Ireland."

"Oh, Bree." Jemma reached over to gently squeeze her hand. "I'm sorry."

"Don't be." She forced a smile. "Learned how to travel across the ocean by myself, didn't I? And I've enjoyed being here with you and Jazz."

"We've loved having you here, too." Jemma's sympathetic gaze only made her feel worse. As if she'd somehow failed the twins.

"Jemma. Bree."

She stiffened when she heard Jake's deep, rumbling voice behind them. She really, really wished she hadn't impulsively jumped a flight to Michigan. Staying here in a room right across the hall from him in the McNally B&B was beyond awkward.

"Jake, sit down." Jemma jumped up from her seat as if someone stuck a pin in her behind. "I'll get you some lemonade."

"I'm fine, Jem." Jake mounted the steps to the gazebo platform. "Don't go to any trouble."

"It's no trouble, Jake," Jemma assured him. "I wanted to thank you again for making the trip here for my wedding. I know you were just here this past June, but I'm so happy you were able to stand in for our father to escort me down the aisle."

"I was glad to do it," Jake assured her. "I like Garth; he's a good guy. Better than your first husband."

"A worm is better than Randal." Jemma let out a wry laugh. "But thanks to Garth, Randal has left me and Trey alone, which is all I ever wanted."

"Glad to hear it." Jake dropped into the chair beside her, his elbow lightly brushing her arm. Bree moved away, feeling burned by his fleeting touch.

"I better check on Trey." Jemma ducked out, leaving them alone.

Bree wanted to call her back but obviously couldn't blame Jemma for wanting to check on her young son. Bree kept her gaze on the vast lake. If one didn't know better, it would be easy to mistake it for the Irish Sea.

Silence stretched long and tense between them.

"I'll be heading back to Kalamazoo in the morning." Bree tucked a curl behind her ear in a nervous gesture. "After I help your sister with breakfast."

Jake was silent for a moment. "You don't have to help Jemma cook, she doesn't mind."

"It's the least I can do after dropping in without an invitation, isn't it?" Bree didn't dare look at Jake, fearing he'd see the dejection in her gaze. "And I like to cook, the way she does. Making a full Irish here in Michigan has been fun, even though nothing compares to the rashers back home." She remembered how much Jake liked Ireland's bacon.

How wonderful the two intense weeks they'd spent together touring castles, the Blarney Stone, and the County Wicklow mountains.

Jake lifted a hand. "Whatever makes you happy."

He certainly didn't make her happy, and wasn't that the

real heart of the issue? "Thanks a mil for playing tour guide for the past couple of days, McNally Bay is a lovely town."

Again, Jake didn't respond, his tendency to remain silent grating on her nerves. She took a sip of her lemonade, wishing for what seemed like the hundredth time that she hadn't come.

Bad enough to know Jake didn't fancy her and planned to move on, but so much worse to prolong the agony. It was well past time to move forward with her own life. One that didn't include the handsome American.

All the McNallys were good-looking, coming from some sort of incredible Irish gene pool, but in her opinion, Jake was the most handsome of them all. His brown hair shimmered with gold highlights that came naturally from the sun, and his dark eyes, similar to Jemma's, were intense. He was tall, rangy yet strong.

And the wrong man for a homebody like her.

"It's not home," Jake finally responded. "Not the way the Murphy Farm is for you, Quinn, and your father."

"What does feel like home to you, then?" She turned in her seat to look at him, but he was watching the sun drop lower over the lake.

"I don't really have a place that feels like home."

His words made her feel incredibly sad for him. It wasn't the first time he'd downplayed his connection to McNally Bay. Bree found it odd, considering three of his five siblings had settled in the area. Why wouldn't McNally Bay feel like home to him?

"Home is where your family is."

He shrugged and finally met her gaze. "Sometimes, but not always. Would you be willing to let me hitch a ride with you to the airport in the morning?"

Her pulse gave a betraying thump of anticipation, and

she struggled to keep her voice level. "Coming back to Collinstown with me, are you?"

"Only to get my things." He turned away, gazing out toward the lake. "I left a few items behind in the cottage."

Deep down, she'd known he couldn't stay long in the small cottage on her father's property. By her last calculation, he had about four weeks left to spend in Ireland before he'd have to move on.

She'd tried to offer him the idea of getting a two-year work visa as her father would have gladly offered to employ Jake on the farm, but he'd declined.

Unwilling to extend his time in Ireland for her. Or her family.

"If you don't mind," he repeated when she didn't respond.

"Grand to ride together. Saves on petrol." She drained her lemonade glass and stood. No way was she going to sit here with Jake to watch the sun set as if they were some sort of romantic couple. Maybe they were once, but not anymore. "See you in the morning."

He opened his mouth as if to say something, but she didn't linger. Instead, she edged past him and carried her empty glass inside.

"Everything okay?" Jemma asked as she entered the kitchen.

"Brilliant." Bree forced a smile. "We're heading back to Kalamazoo in the morning, after breakfast. I'll be down bright and early to help out again."

"You really don't have to help me cook breakfast," Jemma protested. "Although, you do an amazing job. Thanks for teaching me a few new tricks."

She smiled, a genuine smile for what felt like the first

time over the past few days. "You're more than welcome. And like you, I find cooking relaxing."

Jemma impulsively gave Bree a big hug. "Jake's an idiot," she whispered fiercely.

Tears pricked Bree's eyes. "Go on now. No reason we can't be friends."

"Yeah," Jemma agreed. She stepped back and swiped at her face. "Friends."

"Come for a visit sometime," she offered. "You, Garth, and Trey are welcome on the Murphy Equestrian Farm any time. Jazz and Dalton, too."

The invite made Jemma smile. "Don't think I won't take you up on that offer. It's been a dream of mine to see Ireland, the country my great-grandparents came from."

"Anytime, truly." It felt like the least she could do for the McNally twins. "See you in the morning."

Bree left, heading through the dining room and the great room, one that reminded her of some of the old Irish mansions that managed to survive the revolutionary rise against England. She was awed by the great stone fireplace, with tall elegant silver candlesticks framing the painting of the Cliffs of Moher from County Clare. The thick cherry-wood furniture, the grand curved staircase leading to the second-story bedrooms, six of them all decorated with different colors, were just as amazing. Jemma had given her the rose room, which she found lovely.

She approached the grand curved staircase now, enjoying the fact that a bit of Ireland was here in Michigan's McNally Bay.

It seemed appropriate considering Jake McNally would take a small piece of her heart with him when he left Ireland for good.

EVERY CELL in his body urged Jake to follow Bree, but his muscles remained frozen in place.

She shouldn't be here. *He* shouldn't be here. How had he messed things up so badly?

Just under five months ago, he'd flown from Canada to Dublin, leaving a pretty blonde behind. He thought for a moment, trying to remember her name. Katie? No Kayla? Karin? Something like that.

Whatever. It didn't matter. None of them did. He enjoyed spending time with women, and he had never lied to them about his intention to move on when his current project or investment opportunity was completed. Yet somehow every woman he met decided they were the one to change him. To be the one to convince him to put down roots.

To make him realize what he was missing.

They were wrong. There was no way to save him. No way to rescue him from himself. The quicker the women he met understood that, the less likely they would be hurt by his inevitable goodbye.

Like Bree.

He stared vacantly at Lake Michigan, a hollow feeling in his chest. Oddly, leaving Bree Murphy was bothering him in a way he'd never experienced before. Maybe because he'd enjoyed the few weeks he'd sporadically spent in Ireland over the past five months. The moment he'd stopped in at the Murphy Equestrian Farm, he'd felt as if he'd recognized the place. As if the DNA embedded deep in his cells from his Irish ancestors had sprung to life.

But his time in Ireland was over. Frankly, he'd stayed longer than he should have, using up sixty-five of the ninety days his visa allowed. The moment Dark Rogue had won his first two races, Jake had known his project of rejuvenating the Murphy Farm was complete. But he'd continued to come and go between England, where his visa allowed him to stay a full 180 days, to Ireland. He'd also invited Bree to accompany him to Jazz's wedding in June, a mistake as she'd begun to act as if they were a couple. He'd left, spending weeks at a time in Berkshire, England, then had stopped back in Ireland again, before returning to McNally Bay for Jemma's wedding mid-August.

Having Bree show up unexpectedly the day after the wedding had forced him to stick around in McNally Bay for an additional couple of days, playing tour guide for Bree the way she had taken him through Dublin, various castles, and the mountains of County Wicklow.

Long after the sun disappeared below the horizon, he roused himself to head back inside. It was both a relief and an impending sense of doom to know he would be leaving with Bree in the morning.

He'd miss his siblings, but he was determined to move on to his next adventure. He'd been toying with the idea of heading to Florence, Italy. There was a café and villa that he believed might be a decent investment.

Besides, he'd never been to Florence and thought it would be a great place to spend the last three and a half weeks that remained on his visa.

Jake headed inside, making his way to the green room Jemma had given him. He paused outside Bree's door, listening for what he wasn't sure, before moving on.

He didn't sleep well that night, but when he heard Bree's door open across the hallway, he found himself shooting up and out of bed.

After a quick shower, he packed his duffel bag so they could hit the road right after breakfast. Then he headed down to the dining area where he found Jazz and Dalton enjoying coffee.

"Jake!" Jazz jumped up to give him a quick hug. "Jemma told us you're leaving today."

"Yeah." He returned her hug, then stepped back. Long goodbyes made him uncomfortable. "Not sure when I'll be back now that the wedding madness is over."

"Don't count Jeremy and Trina out yet," Jazz warned, dropping into the seat across from her husband. "It's only a matter of time before they'll make it official. I'm convinced there will be one more ceremony in the wings yet this year."

He tried not to groan as he took the seat beside Jazz. "At least Jeremy won't need me to walk him down the aisle."

"Ha, ha." Jazz elbowed him in the ribs. "You're so not funny."

"Not true. I'm hilarious." He glanced around. "Where can I get a cup of tea?"

Jazz lifted a brow. "From the kitchen. Help yourself."

He scowled, realizing his sister wasn't going to wait on him as if he were a B&B guest. Since Bree wasn't seated at one of the tables, he felt certain she was working with Jemma in the kitchen.

His sister's not-so-subtle attempt to push him at Bree wasn't enough to stop him from seeking the caffeine he desperately needed. Bracing himself, he went into the kitchen to find Jemma and Bree discussing a new recipe for rhubarb and walnut bread.

"Hi, Jake." Jemma's cheeks were pink from the heat of the stove. "What can I get for you?"

"Tea, if you don't mind." He noticed Bree avoided his direct gaze. She was beautiful when she wore her long, naturally curly dark hair loose around her shoulders, and this morning her blue eyes seemed incredibly bright. She still had the power to steal his breath. If he were a different kind of guy . . . but he wasn't.

"I have the kettle on." Jemma pushed a small wooden box full of different teas across the counter. "Take your pick, I'll bring out some hot water for you shortly."

"Thanks." He chose the strongest black tea she had, along with a cup and saucer, then retreated back to the dining room.

Man, it was going to be a long drive to Kalamazoo.

Breakfast went by quickly, especially since Bree hid in the kitchen the entire time. When everyone had finished eating, and the kitchen was cleaned up to Bree and Jemma's high standards, it was time to hit the road.

"I'll be down in a minute." Bree headed up to her room, returning with her small carry-on bag. He'd been impressed she hadn't overpacked.

"Goodbye, Bree. Jake." Jemma hugged them both. "I'll call you soon, Bree."

"I'll look forward to it," Bree responded.

Jake wanted to know what they were planning to discuss, then reminded himself it was none of his business. He carried his duffel out to Bree's rental and stashed both of their bags in the trunk.

Bree held out the keys, her gaze hidden behind large sunglasses. "Would you mind driving? I was a wreck driving here on the wrong side of the road."

"Hey, at least our roads are wide enough for two cars." He flashed a quick grin as he plucked the keys from her hand, opened the passenger side door for her, then went around to slide in behind the wheel.

"We'll need petrol." Bree buckled her seat belt. "I managed to get lost, took a wrong turn out of the airport, and ended up in Battle Creek rather than McNally Bay."

"Not a problem." He was glad she didn't seem to be super upset with him. Maybe the drive to Kalamazoo wouldn't be as awful as he'd anticipated.

He headed into town, secretly amazed at the never-ending stream of tourists roaming around this late in August. A lot had changed in McNally Bay since the last time he'd spent the summer here, twelve years ago.

The gas station/convenience store wasn't far. He pulled in next to the pump and began filling the tank.

"I'm going inside for a few minutes." Bree didn't wait for him to respond but left the car and disappeared inside the mini-mart.

When the tank was full, he paid for the gas via his credit card and waited for Bree. After a few minutes, he sighed and followed her into the building. Maybe she was loading up on snacks for the long plane trip back to Ireland.

He didn't see her but figured she might be using the restroom. Perusing the shelves, he considered the snack options.

After pulling a bag of almonds from the rack, he froze when he heard a raspy voice behind him.

"That nosy family is looking for evidence."

Jake's mouth went dry, his pulse spiking with fear. It was a voice from the past. One he'd hoped to avoid, forever.

"They won't find it," a second nasally voice said.

"You'd better hope not."

"It doesn't matter, we'll be fine as long as we keep our mouths shut."

"You have more to lose than I do."

The brief conversation ended when the two men rounded the corner and left the convenience store.

Jake slowly turned but couldn't see the two men as they left, as they were hidden behind the post. By the time he'd made his way closer to the window, they were well out of sight. Still, he felt as if he'd stepped back through a time machine to twelve years ago.

To the summer that had changed him forever.

His breath hitched in his throat as a shiver of fear washed over him.

Everyone thought McNally Bay was a pretty little tourist town, harmless except for the occasional drug bust and other petty crime.

But Jake knew better.

McNally Bay had a dark underbelly. And the deeply buried secrets upon which the idyllic town had grown into a well-known tourist destination were exactly what had kept him far away all these years.

He couldn't wait to get out of there, once and for all.

J ake remained stubbornly silent as they headed toward the Kalamazoo airport, his expression grim after they'd stopped for petrol in town.

"After picking up your things at the cottage, where are you off to next?" She kept her tone light as if it didn't bother her in the least that he was moving on from Ireland.

He lifted a shoulder. "There's a café and villa in Florence, Italy, I'd like to look at. From the photos online, it may be a good investment."

Florence, Italy. She swallowed hard and forced a smile. "I hear it's lovely there." She hadn't been to Italy; the only major trips she'd taken were the ferry to England related to horse racing and her two trips here to McNally Bay. The Murphy Farm's finances hadn't allowed for luxuries such as international travel. Her visit to McNally Bay in June had been her first overseas flight, and Jake had paid for that one out of his frequent flyer miles.

Why, oh, why had she come a second time?

Jake didn't respond but kept his attention centered on

the road. It seemed there was something more bothering him, but she squelched the urge to ask.

He wasn't likely to confide in her now, not after being so bloody taciturn the past couple of days. The strain between them made her feel as if they were complete strangers instead of two people who'd spent weeks together laughing, joking, watching the races, and sharing meals while touring the hot spots in England and, of course, Ireland.

She'd taken him to all her favorite places. Had shared all her secret hopes and dreams.

Yet in the end, she'd been silly enough to think that a little Irish country mouse such as herself would be enough to attract a world traveler like Jake McNally.

She told herself she'd be better off once he headed for Italy.

After what seemed like forever, they reached the airport and turned over the keys to her rental car. She had a return ticket going through Chicago to Dublin, and of course, Jake had booked for the same flight. It didn't surprise her to learn he had a seat in first class.

They sat in the terminal with a vacant spot between them, a gap that felt wider than the Irish Sea. In an effort to distract herself, she pulled out her tablet to read. She loved murder mysteries and did her best to ignore Jake, who was slouched in his seat with his head back and eyes closed.

No doubt pretending to be asleep so he wouldn't have to talk to anyone.

Especially to her.

Fine. She didn't want to talk to him either. So she'd made a mistake in following him to McNally Bay. It wouldn't be the first time she'd made a bloody fool of herself.

But it would hopefully be the last. She'd learned her lesson and was done with American men.

Maybe all men. Truly now, they weren't worth the heartache.

When the call came over the speakers announcing all first-class passengers could begin to board, Jake opened his eyes, stretched, and slowly rose to his feet.

"I have to go, but I'm sure I'll see you later," he said without smiling.

Not if I see you first. She forced a smile. "Yeah, maybe. Take care of yourself, Jake."

There was a slight hesitation before he responded. "You, too, Brianna."

It took every ounce of willpower she possessed not to stand and hug him one last time. And she couldn't help but watch as he ambled over to take his place in the queue to board the airplane. When he disappeared from view, she let out a heavy sigh. If she'd had the funds, she'd have changed her ticket to a later time, but while their farm was currently running in the black, she couldn't bring herself to squander quid as if it could be found in a pot at the end of a rainbow. Paying for the ticket to come here where she wasn't wanted had proven frivolous enough.

Remorse hit hard. She closed her eyes, wishing she could turn back the clock, make a better, less impulsive decision.

Enough. The only way to get through the long journey home was to focus on seeing her family again. Her dad and Quinn would be glad to have her back.

They had Dark Rogue now and a future on their equestrian farm. She didn't need anything more.

Glancing at her boarding pass, she remembered there was a two-hour layover in Chicago. Even though they were on the same flight, she remembered the airport being huge, so she hoped it wouldn't be too difficult to avoid further contact with Jake.

And if her heart ached for him, it was her own fault for giving him the power to hurt her. For being foolish enough to think she had anything to offer the man who refused to put down roots.

She stood, slung her carry-on over her shoulder and moved closer to the gate to mingle with the other passengers who were also waiting to board. As she waited for her group to be called, her phone rang.

Frowning, she looked down at the screen, then quickly picked it up. "Jemma? What's wrong?"

"Bree, I'm so glad you answered. Are you on the plane yet?"

The strain in Jemma's voice filled her with concern. "No, why? What's happened?"

"I tripped and fell over Goldie, you remember our Goldendoodle puppy? I'm afraid I may have broken my wrist. Would you mind coming back to the B and B? I hate to impose on you, Bree, but you're the only one I can think of who can take my place cooking breakfast in the kitchen for our guests. Jazz, well, she's okay with making eggs and such, but completely hopeless when it comes to baking. If you can't come"—there was a catch in her voice—"we may lose our business."

"Yes, of course, I'll return to cook for you." She glanced over to where passengers were slowly making their way on board the plane. "Jake's already seated in first class, do you want me to let him know?"

"I tried his cell, but he didn't answer." Jemma's voice sounded tense, as if she were gritting her teeth against the pain. "Don't bother Jake, I'm pretty sure he won't want to stick around anyway. But I would be grateful for your help,

Bree. Please know I'll repay the cost of your ticket and provide a salary for the time you spend cooking breakfast. I know that this is a huge imposition, but I don't know what else to do. We have a wedding scheduled this weekend and the next one after that, and I can't stand the idea of canceling on them."

"Don't be daft, you can't cancel two weddings! I don't mind lending a hand. It will take me a while to pick up another car and drive back into town." She was grateful she only had a carry-on, there wouldn't be an issue with her luggage flying to Dublin without her. "I'll be back in McNally Bay as soon as possible."

"Garth is taking me to the local clinic for X-rays, so if we're not here when you arrive, make yourself at home." Another pause, before Jemma added, "Thank you, Bree. I owe you big time."

"No, it's the other way around. See you soon." After disconnecting from the call, she slid the phone into her bag. She felt bad for Jemma, but the abrupt turn of events made her feel at peace.

It felt good to turn her back on the gate. To walk away, leaving regret and shame behind.

The more distance she put between herself and Jake, the lighter her step. She'd have to call her dad and Quinn to let them know she was staying on in the states a while longer.

At least this time, she knew she wouldn't have to put up with Jake being at the B&B, with his grumpy face and long brooding silence. It was time to put her life back on track, move on from her mistakes. Which would be easier to do being half the world away from Jake McNally and his new café and villa in Florence, Italy.

Especially since he'd made it clear he had no plans to return to McNally Bay anytime soon, if ever.

Despite his bone-weary exhaustion, Jake kept hearing the brief conversation between the two men in the gas station, feeling more and more certain that they were the same men he'd seen twelve years ago. Was he making a mistake leaving McNally Bay? Was it finally time to tell the police what he'd witnessed? When they'd mentioned *that nosy family*, had they meant the McNallys? It seemed likely. If he left, would they decide to go after his sisters?

The possibility made his gut clench with worry.

He watched the stream of passengers going past his seat, searching for Bree. He should have mentioned something about what he'd overheard during their drive but hadn't. Now for some odd reason, he wanted her opinion. When the crowd dwindled and he didn't see her, he frowned.

Had he missed her? He didn't see how that was possible considering he was in the front row of the first-class seating and had a clear view of every person edging past him.

Moments later, he heard her name over the PA system.

"Passenger Brianna Murphy, please report to gate number twenty-three. Your flight is ready to depart."

The knot in his gut tightened to the point he almost doubled over in pain. Where was she? Had something happened? Or had she simply taken a last stop in the restroom without realizing she might miss her flight?

Two flight attendants stood near the cockpit, whispering. Then one shrugged and reached out to close the door.

"No!" He leaped out of his seat. "Aren't you going to wait for Brianna Murphy?"

The attendant eyed him warily. "Sir, I need you to return to your seat."

Panic hit low and hard. "I just need to go out there to

check on her. She isn't a seasoned traveler, and I think she might just be in the restroom."

The attendant lifted a brow. "And you're going to go inside the ladies' room to find her? I don't think so. Now please sit down. The captain has given us the go-ahead to close the cabin door and prepare for takeoff."

"You can't do that, Bree isn't on the plane, yet." He knew he was behaving irrationally, but he couldn't seem to shake it off.

"Sir, don't make me call security."

He scowled and pulled out his phone. He'd missed a call from Jemma, which was odd, but there wasn't anything from Bree. He quickly called her, doing his best to stare down the flight attendant as he waited for Bree to pick up. "One more minute isn't going to hurt."

"Sir, I'm not going to ask you again." The underlying note of steel in her tone convinced him that he wasn't going to win this one.

Bree didn't answer, his call going through to voice mail.

"Sir, please sit down!" The flight attendant was losing her patience with him.

He hesitated for just a moment, before grabbing his duffel out of the overhead bin and slinging it over his shoulder. "Fine, I'm out of here."

"Wait! You can't just leave . . ."

He ignored her sputtered protest, brushing past her to exit the plane. He was only halfway up the ramp when he heard the airplane door closing behind him with a soft snick.

Retracing his steps, Jake returned to the terminal gate area, which was now fairly empty. He raked his gaze over the few people standing around, searching for Brianna.

Where in the world was she?

He called her phone again, but she still didn't answer. This time, he left a message. "Bree, it's Jake. Where are you? You missed your flight, but I can help you get on a different one. Please call me back."

He slid the phone into his pocket and headed over toward the closest pair of restrooms. He stood outside the women's room until a young woman came out.

"Excuse me, could you please go back inside to find my —er—girlfriend? Her name is Brianna Murphy. I think she might be sick or something."

"Oh, uh, sure." The young woman looked concerned as she turned around to go back inside.

He waited for endless seconds for her to return with Brianna.

But the young lady returned alone.

"I'm sorry, but there's no one named Brianna Murphy in there."

"Are you sure?"

"I'm sure." The young woman was looking at him with an expression of compassion mixed with pity. "I'm sorry, but maybe your girlfriend decided to go—somewhere else." Her subtle meaning wasn't lost on him.

In other words, maybe Brianna had dumped him.

"Yeah. Thanks." He turned away, his mind whirling. It just didn't make any sense.

Unless—had Bree decided to take a different flight altogether? No denying they hadn't spoken much on the drive to Kalamazoo. His fault, as he'd been preoccupied with the ghosts from his past.

Maybe she despised the thought of flying back through Chicago to Dublin on the same plane he was on to the point that she'd made a snap decision to change flights.

Not that he could entirely blame her.

But as he made his way back through the terminal, he realized it wasn't like Bree to waste money. The entire Murphy family was frugal by nature. No matter what her personal feelings were toward him, she wouldn't simply throw away a perfectly good plane ticket.

Worry morphed into downright concern. Missing her flight like this was totally out of character for her. Bree would never do something like this without a really good reason.

He tried her cell again, without success. Then he tried Jemma, but she didn't answer either. Finally, he tried Jazz, without success.

It was as if Brianna had disappeared along with his family.

He crossed over to the closest desk manned by an attendant. "I need to know if Brianna Murphy is on another flight."

The woman barely glanced at him. "I'm sorry, but I can't give out passenger information."

Logically, he knew she was right, but he was fast losing patience with the bureaucracy. "Listen, she missed the flight we were on together, and I'm worried about her. So please, just tell me if she's on another flight. You don't have to tell me where she's going or which flight she's on, I just need to know she's safe."

"Sir, I really can't . . ."

"What if she's been kidnapped? Or worse?" He didn't normally go to the worst-case scenario, but his internal desperation couldn't be ignored. "Can you see the headlines? *Pretty Irish Citizen Kidnapped from Kalamazoo Airport, Staff Refused to Help Find Her.* Because trust me, I'll make sure every television station knows you wouldn't help me. Now, will you please just check!"

"Okay, okay." The woman's fingers flew across her keyboard. After staring at her screen for several minutes, she slowly shook her head. "I'm sorry sir, but she was a no-show on flight seven fifty-four to Chicago, final destination Dublin, Ireland."

"I told you she wasn't on the flight." His pulse spiked with fear. "You're saying she isn't on another flight?"

The woman's gaze mirrored his concern. "She is not on another flight."

"Will you page her again?"

This time, she didn't argue but picked up the handset. "Will passenger Brianna Murphy please come to gate twenty-three in terminal B. Brianna Murphy, please come to gate twenty-three in terminal B."

He turned from the desk, scanning the crowds, hoping, praying Brianna would be rushing toward him.

But after five minutes, then ten, there was nothing.

"Thank you." Moving away from the desk, he pulled out his phone to call Brianna again. The call went to voice mail, and he resisted the urge to throw the device against the wall in frustration.

Maybe she really had dumped him. Like left the airport to go catch a flight out of Battle Creek or Lansing instead. It was the only possibility that made sense.

He turned back to the desk to ask about the next available flight to Chicago when his phone rang. Looking at the number, a wave of relief hit him hard. Bree!

"Where are you?"

"Where are you?" she countered. "Aren't you airborne by now?"

She had ditched him on purpose. He swallowed a surge of anger. "No, I'm not. I was worried when you didn't get on the plane. I'm standing in the middle of the terminal. Where are you?"

"Driving back to McNally Bay." Bree's voice didn't sound upset or angry, which for some reason annoyed him. "Didn't you get Jemma's message?"

His heart jumped in his chest. "No, I had a missed call but no message. I tried her back, but she didn't answer. Why? What happened? Is she okay? Garth? Trey?" The idea of something happening to his young nephew made him feel anxious all over again.

"She's fine, other than a sprained or possibly broken wrist. Apparently, she tripped over Goldie."

His heart settled back into a normal rhythm. "I'm sorry to hear that, but what does that have to do with you?"

"She asked me to come back to help cook breakfasts for her." Brianna's voice held a disturbing note of cheerfulness. "Can't very well cancel the two upcoming weddings they have scheduled, can she?"

"I guess not." The possibility that Bree had decided to stay longer in McNally Bay had never entered his mind. Although he realized now that it made sense. The guests at the B&B raved about the breakfasts and the quaint atmosphere overlooking the lake. They also enjoyed spending time in the small town.

He was one of the few who knew the truth.

"Maybe I should come back, too." The words popped out of his mouth before he could hold them back.

There was a slight pause. "No need for that, Jemma doesn't expect you to return."

She only spoke the truth, but the comment stung. The conversation he'd overheard at the gas station echoed through his mind.

It doesn't matter, we'll be fine as long as we keep our mouths shut.

You have more to lose than I do.

"Sorry to worry you over nothing." Bree's light tone bugged him. "I hope you can catch another flight, Jake. In fact, if you'd like to head straight to Florence, it's no problem for us to ship any items you have in the cottage. Would be a waste of quid to fly to Ireland for that."

The cottage was the original home of the Murphys' farm. Seamus Murphy, Bree's father, grew up in the cottage, then built the new home shortly after he'd met and married Brianna's mother, Maggie. Bree's mother died of cancer seven years ago, so Seamus, Quinn, and Bree shared the main house now.

Seamus had confided in him that there was more than enough land on the farm to build another home, if needed. A not-so-subtle hint related to Jake's future with Brianna. A hint that had sent icy cold water sliding down to his feet.

"Jake? Still there?"

He shook off the memories. "Yes, I'm here. How long do you think you'll be staying in McNally Bay?"

"I don't know, depends on Jemma's wrist. She's hoping the injury is only a sprain, but if it's broken, could be a month or two."

Again, the way she sounded, well, downright *happy* about the whole thing, puzzled him.

"Listen, Jake, I need to get back on the highway. I pulled over to ring you back, but I want to be back at the B and B in time to help get things ready for the morning."

"Yeah, I know." He couldn't explain why he was reluctant to let her go. "I'm glad you're okay, Bree."

"Why wouldn't I be?"

"No reason. I was confused, that's all." He didn't want to

explain the crazy panic attack he'd had while trying to figure out what had happened to cause her to miss her flight.

"Goodbye, Jake. I hope you find what you're looking for in Florence." She disconnected from the call, leaving him standing in the middle of the airport feeling like an idiot.

Bree was fine, he'd gotten off the plane for nothing. And she was right, it did make more sense to fly directly to Florence rather than taking the detour through Ireland. Why hadn't he considered asking her to ship his things to Italy in the first place?

Because he'd wanted to return to the Murphys' farm. To say goodbye in person.

There was nothing keeping him from moving on to the next phase of his life. He turned and stared at the woman still standing behind the counter.

His feet didn't move. He couldn't bring himself to go ahead and book another flight.

As much as he'd made it his mission to avoid McNally Bay, he knew couldn't just leave. The voices he'd overheard had shocked him to his core. After all these years, it never really occurred to him that the two men would still be living there.

And he couldn't seem to worry about his siblings being in possible danger. *That nosy family is looking for evidence.*

He didn't like it. The town had been named for the McNallys. What other family could they have been talking about?

He only had one option. Return to McNally Bay, at least for a while.

If nothing else, he needed to be sure that the ghosts of the past stayed deeply buried, where they belonged.

3

Bree pulled into the small parking lot in front of the B&B with a strange sense of relief. Jazz came rushing out to meet with her.

"Thank you so much for helping us out, Bree." Jemma's twin sister, as dark as Jemma was blonde, enveloped her in a big hug. "We couldn't do this without you."

"Go on now, it's fine, that's what friends are for, isn't it? Have you heard from Jemma?"

"Yes. No broken bones, but a bad sprain. They've put her wrist in a brace with instructions not to use it for at least a week. Once the swelling is down, they want her to go to Kalamazoo for an MRI scan." Jazz's green eyes clouded with worry. "If the tendons have been damaged, she may need surgery."

"Surgery? I sure hope not." Bree felt bad for what Jemma might be going through. "Best to think positive, isn't it?"

"Yes, absolutely." Jazz's smile didn't quite reach her eyes. "Come inside, we've set aside the master suite for you."

"The master suite?" Bree was taken aback. "Why not the rose room?"

"The master is close to the kitchen, which makes it easier for you." Jazz led the way inside. "Besides, all the rooms are booked this upcoming weekend for the wedding."

That made sense. "The master will be grand. I'd like to take a look at what Jemma has in the kitchen, take a quick inventory of what I may need for the morning."

"Sure thing. Jemma should be back soon, you may want to talk to her about what she has planned."

"I will." Bree looked into the fridge, took note of the fresh cranberries, wondering if Jemma had planned to use them for muffins. "I want to make a list."

Jazz handed her a pad of paper and a pencil.

She hadn't taken many notes when she heard the sound of the front door. Assuming Garth had brought Jemma back, she called, "I'm in the kitchen."

"I figured as much." Jake's deep voice knocked her back a step.

She gaped at him, her mind whirling. She would have bet Dark Rogue's latest winnings that Jake would have gotten on the next flight out of Kalamazoo without looking back. "What are you doing here?"

He dropped his duffel, shrugged, and slid his hands into the front pockets of his khaki slacks. "I had already missed my flight, thought it might be a good idea to check on Jemma and Trey."

She stared at him. "But—you were supposed to be on your way to Italy."

"Not yet." He glanced around. "Where is Jemma anyway?"

She gripped the counter to keep her steady. "Still at the hospital. Jazz says they didn't find any broken bones, just a bad sprain."

"That's good to hear."

"Yes." The inane conversation was driving her mad. She couldn't believe Jake had followed her back here. "How long are you planning to stay in McNally Bay?"

"I'm not sure."

She ground her teeth together, battling a wave of frustration. "I don't understand why you've come, Jake. You've made it clear you don't think of McNally Bay as your home."

"I know, but I wanted to check on Jemma, make sure she's all right."

Since when? She bit her tongue and let it go, knowing there was nothing to be gained by pushing the issue. There was no doubt Jake cared about his family, especially his youngest sisters, but to return to McNally Bay just to check on Jemma seemed a flimsy excuse.

She felt certain Jake wouldn't stay for long. A day or two at the most.

It wasn't the end of the world to put up with him for another couple of days.

"Jake, I'm here to help her with breakfast, and I can watch Trey, too. No need to put your plans for Florence on hold."

"I'm not." His swift denial didn't ring true.

"What if someone buys the villa out from underneath you?"

He shrugged. "If it's still available, that's fine. If not, I'll find something else to invest in."

Of that she had no doubt. Jake McNally had a knack for making oodles of quid wherever he went. The way he'd turned the Murphy Equestrian Farm around with Dark Rogue certainly proved it.

She wanted to scream at him to leave her alone. Couldn't he see she didn't want him there?

"If you don't like it here, why did you come?" She

couldn't hold on to her patience. "I'll be fine on my own. Your sisters are grand."

He glanced at her. "Yes, Jemma and Jazz are great. And so are you for agreeing to help out like this."

"Then why?" She felt a desperate need to convince him to leave.

Jake was silent for several moments. "I know I'm sending you mixed messages," he admitted.

"Do you?"

He winced. "I'm not doing it on purpose. I was all set to fly to Florence, but I just couldn't seem to do it." He shot a glance at her. "When it came down to it, I couldn't bear to leave you, Bree."

Her heart thumped crazily in her chest, and she inwardly groaned. Jake at his most charming was difficult to ignore. "Bullocks," she retorted. "I'm thinking you're not used to women letting you go without a fight."

"That's not true," he argued. But she noticed a flash of guilt cross his features.

"Yes, it is. Didn't you mention coming to Ireland from Toronto? There was a woman you'd left behind, Katerina, wasn't it? She begged you not to go, didn't she?"

When the tips of his ears turned red, she knew she'd nailed it.

"Is that what I need to do, then? Beg you not to go to Italy? Beg you to give a relationship between us a chance?" She took a step forward, leaning in close and lowering her voice. "Is that what you need to hear from me, Jake? How much I care about you?"

It was his turn to shift from one foot to the other, but he surprised her by reaching out to capture her hand. "I'm not going to deny I like hearing those words from you."

His fingers radiated heat, and it took all her willpower

not to pull away from the scorching awareness.

"Okay, then. If you want the truth, I'll give it to you. I care about you, Jacob McNally. And I would like nothing more than to be in a relationship with you."

She fully expected him to let her go, pushing her away the way he had when she'd arrived at McNally Bay without an invitation.

But he gently squeezed her hand. "I should be scared, but I'm not. Because I care about you, too, Bree."

No. *NO!* This was not going the way she'd planned. He was supposed to run away, hopping the first flight to Florence, or England, or Toronto, or anywhere that wasn't McNally Bay. "What are you saying?"

"That I'm willing to give a relationship with you a try." His response didn't radiate confidence, yet it still managed to rock her back on her heels.

Words failed her. This wasn't what she wanted. Well, truthfully, it was, but not like this. Not in a way that made it clear Jake wasn't sure he had what it took to make a relationship work.

Not when she still had no idea why he didn't consider McNally Bay to be home in the first place.

Dear heaven above, what had she done?

JAKE WAS surprised by the lack of panic he felt when he'd agreed to be with Bree. Exploring new territory by entering a relationship with her.

Had she sprinkled him with some sort of Celtic faery magic? He didn't believe in such things, but there was no denying that he was acting completely out of character.

Yet for the first time in what seemed like weeks, he felt a

strange sense of peace. It had taken time for his mind to understand what his body was telling him.

He was growing tired of running. Of moving on. Of starting over in a new place with new people.

Yet just thinking about the voices he'd overheard at the gas station earlier that morning made his shoulders knot with tension. Memories of the past made it impossible to relax.

He needed to make sure any possible threat to him wouldn't spill over to his family. Yet, staying in McNally Bay even for a week or two would seem like forever. Especially since he wanted to avoid Main Street. The B&B was nice, but he'd go crazy cooped up there for more than a few days.

And he'd already shown Brianna the few touristy places that he knew about.

"Jake! What on earth are you doing here?"

Jemma's incredulous tone had Bree snatching her hand from his and stepping away, her back pressed up against the kitchen counter behind her. He turned to face Jemma, frowning at her pale skin and the brackets of pain cornering her mouth.

"Here, sit down. You look exhausted." He drew Jemma toward the picnic-style bench seat. He wrapped his arm around her shoulder in a brief hug. "I'm sorry you're hurt, Jem. What happened? Are you sure you're okay?"

She cradled her splinted wrist to her stomach and offered a wan smile. "I will be. Stupid of me to trip over Goldie like that."

The Goldendoodle puppy wasn't very well trained, but Jake wasn't about to point that out. "It could happen to anyone."

"Maybe. But the worst part is the fact that Trey was far more concerned about Goldie than me."

He tried not to smile. "He's almost four; he still thinks you're indestructible."

"I'm not." Jemma caught his gaze. "Jeremy helped me navigate through the hospital system in Kalamazoo and told me I was fortunate not to need surgery."

"Surgery would be rough." A flutter of panic hit his belly. Surgery would mean sticking around for six to eight weeks, maybe longer.

"Tell me about it." Jemma sighed. "I'm grateful for Bree's help. I couldn't think of anyone else who could cook Irish breakfasts in my place."

"I'm happy to lend a hand." Bree took the teakettle off the stove and filled a mug with steaming water and handed her a couple of tea bags to choose from. "You just rest and relax, Jemma. I'll take care of everything."

"Jake? What are you doing here?" Jazz said as she entered the kitchen, sounding just as surprised as Jemma to see him there.

He stifled a sigh. "You think I'm completely heartless? I was worried about Jemma and Trey."

His twin sisters exchanged a look he wasn't able to decipher. Did they suspect that his main reason for returning was something deeper? He didn't want to burden either of them with his problems.

"Of course, you're always welcome here, Jake," Jazz said. "I can put you in the green room for now, but the entire B and B is booked Friday through Sunday for a wedding."

"The green room is fine, but what about Bree?" He glanced at Brianna who was doing her best to stay out of the family dynamics.

Not that he blamed her.

"We've set aside the master suite for Bree since she'll be up early making breakfast each morning," Jazz explained.

"But don't worry, you can always bunk with me and Dalton on Friday and Saturday night. We'll throw together some sort of sleeping area for you."

"Not a problem." He knew Jazz and Dalton were renovating their new home, the old Stevenson place located right next door to the B&B, and much of it was still drywall and particleboard. Yet he didn't mind. He'd slept in worse places than a construction zone.

"Okay, so what can I do to help?" He glanced at Jemma. "I know I'm just as useless as Jazz in the kitchen, but is there something else you need? What about Trey?"

"I can keep an eye on Trey with one arm in a brace, and Garth can help me with him as well," Jemma pointed out. "Thankfully, he starts his pre-K program the Tuesday after Labor Day."

"Dalton can use a hand with our renovations." Jazz dropped onto the seat beside Jemma at the table. "We're also kicking off the very first McNally Bay Autumn Fest fundraiser with all proceeds going toward the cost of supplying a K-9 officer for the Clark County Sheriff's Department."

"Trina has already purchased the K-9 from her own funds," Jemma added. "But the training is very expensive. We're hoping to raise enough money to cover the entire cost of the training along with feeding the K-9 for the first few months. We think the town should help be responsible for the K-9 helping to eradicate any leftover drug issues."

"We're auctioning off a weekend getaway at the B and B as one of the raffle prizes." Jazz's wide smile turned into a frown. "Hopefully, Jemma will be able to cook by then."

Jake wanted to groan. Autumn Fest? It was tempting to offer to pay for the entire K-9 program himself rather than work with the townsfolk on their fundraiser, but he suspected that wouldn't go over very well. It was easy to see Jazz and Jemma were totally into their campaign to raise money for Trina's K-9.

"I'll help too," Bree offered. "With the Autumn Fest, not the renovations."

"I haven't swung a hammer in a long time, but I will do what I can to help with the renovations." Better to work on the old Stevenson place than to be involved in the festival.

He really hoped Jemma wouldn't need surgery. That he wouldn't be stuck here for six to eight endless weeks. Even house renovations couldn't keep him occupied for that long.

He swallowed hard. Had he made a mistake in coming here? In trying to ensure his family's safety and giving a relationship with Bree a chance?

"I need to run to the grocery store." Bree's statement interrupted his thoughts.

"I'll give you a lift," he offered. So much for avoiding Main Street, but the idea of sitting around the B&B was already getting to him.

Bree hesitated, then nodded. "All right." She turned to Jemma. "I'll get everything together tonight so I'm ready for breakfast in the morning."

"I'll help. I still have one good hand." Jemma's expression was wry.

"As long as you don't overdo," Bree admonished. "I'm sure I can handle most of the work."

"Thank you, Bree." Jemma's smile was full of gratitude. "You're amazing to do this for us."

"Don't forget to use the McNally B and B credit card." Jazz handed it to Bree. "As promised, we're paying you a salary for your work, too. And there's no need to worry about dinner tonight, Dalton offered to pick up Chinese for everyone."

"Really, paying me a salary isn't necessary," Bree protested. "Friends help each other out, don't they?"

"We insist," Jemma said firmly. "Without you, we'd likely lose our business."

"Time for Jazz to learn how to cook," Jake teased, trying to lighten things up.

"You could learn, too," Jazz countered, her tone bristling. "In fact, it would do all the McNally men good to learn how to cook and bake like Jemma. It's not just women's work, you know."

He held up his hands in surrender. "Okay, okay. Forget I mentioned it." He caught Bree's gaze. "Ready?"

Bree nodded, and they walked through the great room and back outside. There was a hint of autumn in the air even though all the leaves on the trees were still green. It hit him that he'd never been in McNally Bay long enough to see the leaves change. He and his siblings had only spent their summers here with their grandparents, and the occasional Christmas holiday.

Was it his imagination or were the bottoms of his feet starting to itch?

"I hope Jemma's wrist heals quickly." Bree's expression was serious.

"Agree. I'm glad Jeremy was around to help her get through the medical side of things." It shouldn't have bothered him that Jemma had spoken to Jeremy without so much as leaving him a message about her injury.

It was his own fault that he was distant from his siblings. He knew they joked about his playboy lifestyle and the fact that he didn't stay in one place for very long.

But now he realized just how out of the loop he really was. Bree was closer to Jemma and Jazz than he was.

How messed up was that?

He turned off Highway ZZ and headed down Main Street. The familiar tightening of his neck and shoulder muscles betrayed his discomfort.

Time for him to get over it. He wasn't the naïve twenty-three-year-old kid who'd hidden from danger.

But he couldn't help but glance pointedly at everyone he passed by, instinctively searching for a familiar face.

He pulled into the parking lot of Templeton Grocery. Before he had a chance to turn off the car, Bree was pushing open her passenger side door.

"This may take a while," she warned. "Wouldn't you rather wait out here?"

"I can do that." The interior of the vehicle was too hot with the sun beating in, so he slid out from behind the wheel and headed over to the shade beneath the overhang of the storefront.

The occasional blast of air conditioning felt good when people went in or out of the store. Deciding it was foolish to wait outside, he went into the store and walked past the aisles until he caught sight of Bree.

She was shopping like a woman on a mission, picking through produce as if on the hunt for the perfect fruits and veggies. She scoured every label as if searching for gold. They weren't in a rush, but the inactivity started to chafe.

No way in the world was he going to last even a week in McNally Bay.

Was it possible there was a project somewhere outside of town that might keep him occupied for a bit? Something other than planning the Autumn Festival? He had no desire to get close and chummy with the locals.

Especially the older ones who'd been living here twelve years ago.

He'd convinced himself he had imagined the familiar

voices from the mini-mart when he heard them again.

"We gotta do something to keep that family from poking their nose in our business," the same nasally voice from the previous week sent goose bumps over his arms.

"Not here. Shut up, already," the low, raspy voice said.

Jake left Bree and her cart and casually headed over to the other aisle. Two men, both in their late sixties, were making their way toward the self-service checkout lane. He couldn't tell who they were from the back, other than noting one was taller than the other.

He hesitated, torn with indecision. He didn't want to be caught eavesdropping, but he also needed to get a better look at them. After a long moment, he quickened his pace. The taller, unshaven man only had a couple of items, and he was already swiping them at the register.

Ridiculous beads of sweat prickled at his temples. He ducked behind a shelf full of cereal boxes, willing his pulse to slow down. After taking a deep breath, he looked around the shelf just in time to see the two men leaving the store.

He was going to miss them! Jake quickly skirted several shoppers in an attempt to get close to the large front windows overlooking the parking lot.

As he watched, the two men jumped into a beat-up silver car. Within moments, they were gone.

Jake was too far away to see the license plate number, and the reflection of the sun against the windshield made it impossible to get a good look at the driver. He stood there, battling a wave of helplessness until they were out of sight.

He hadn't yet seen either of their faces, yet he firmly believed one of the two men was the same guy Jake had seen twelve years ago.

The guy who had heartlessly committed cold-blooded murder.

4

_____

Bree was nervous about her role as stand-in breakfast cook for Jemma. She stood in the middle of the aisle, reviewing the planned menu for the next several days over again in her mind. A double check of the items in her cart confirmed she had everything she needed.

Since she didn't know where Jake had wandered off to, she went through the checkout queue on her own, using the B&B credit card to pay for the items. Jake joined her after she'd finished, but he didn't say anything about where he'd been. Yet it was obvious something had put the tension back in his expression.

"Something wrong?" she asked as they walked outside, crossing the parking lot toward their rental.

"No, why?" He sounded irritated, and she knew he was tired from driving to the airport and back.

As was she, but she didn't snap his head off, did she?

With an effort, she kept her voice even. "You look upset." She stood back as he moved the bags from the cart to the boot of the rental. When he finished, she returned the cart to the rack and slid in beside him.

He rolled down the windows to let the cool air in. Her long, curly hair blew into her face, and she wished she'd pulled it back into its customary ponytail to keep the riot of curls under some semblance of control. The humidity of the lake caused her hair to expand so that she looked similar to Goldie, only dark rather than light.

Jake didn't respond for several minutes. She was growing weary of his moodiness. If he didn't want to be in McNally Bay, all he needed to do was to leave.

Frankly, she would have preferred it. Being with Jake wasn't likely to help her relax. Just the opposite.

"I'm fine, just thinking about how I'm going to spend my time while I'm here," he finally admitted.

Ah, so that was it. "Need a project, do you?"

He shot her a quick glance, the corner of his mouth kicking up in a reluctant smile. "Yes. Sitting around doing nothing isn't my style."

"Nor mine," she reminded him. She'd enjoyed working the Murphy Farm and had also juggled a part-time job at the corner pub on the weekends. When they'd gone to England to race Rogue, she'd given up her position at the pub because things had gotten busy around the farm. She'd planned to return in the winter months when there was no racing, although there was also less tourism to require her services. "Cooking breakfast isn't going to keep me occupied for an entire day either."

"You offered to help with the Autumn Fest."

And he hadn't. "Yes, but that isn't the same as running the farm back home."

Jake nodded thoughtfully. "Okay, I'll see if I can find something to give both of us something to do."

His comment surprised her. It was the first time he'd ever included her in his plans, and she wasn't sure what to make of it.

Sure, they'd worked together on Rogue, but that was only because she and her father had horses who'd raced the circuit in the past. Jake had been, and still was, just another investor. The real work was done by the Murphys.

This new prospect felt very different.

She warned herself not to read anything into his plan. Especially since she didn't really believe he had it in him to be in a relationship. After all, he was treating this stay in McNally Bay as some sort of temporary prison term. As if once he'd done his time, he'd be free to move on with his life.

Heading to Florence or some other exciting location. Wherever Jake's next investment project took him.

She, in turn, would head home to Ireland. Back to living on the Murphy Farm with Quinn and her dad. She had no desire to live like a nomad, going from one location to the next, with no roots and no real future plans.

More proof that she and Jake were all wrong for each other. Any sort of relationship between them was hopeless. She wanted to settle down, have a family. Live in Ireland near the Murphy Farm.

Jake would never be happy living in one place for the rest of his life, and that was something she needed to keep in the forefront of her mind.

She cared about him, it was difficult not to, but she absolutely could not afford to fall any further in love with him.

When they returned to the B&B, Jake carried the groceries inside, then left her in the kitchen alone to head over to Jazz and Dalton's home located to the west of the B&B.

Bree did as much prep work as she could for the following morning's breakfast, making batter for the cranberry-walnut muffins and the lemon-poppy seed bread. She thought it would be better to get up early to make the brown bread fresh. When she finished, she took time to clean the kitchen so it was as spotless as Jemma had left it.

Within minutes of wiping down the countertops, Dalton, Jazz, and Jake arrived carrying large white bags of Chinese takeout.

Her mouth watered at the enticing aroma of sesame seeds, soy sauce, and garlic. The emotional ups and downs of the day had worn her down, and she wanted nothing more than to fill her stomach and then crawl into bed to get some badly needed sleep. "Looks brilliant. Where are Jemma, Garth, and Trey?"

"They'll be here soon," Jazz told her. "Garth took Trey fishing so Jemma could rest. They're getting cleaned up now."

Bree knew they lived in the newly built apartment above the large four-car garage, using an intercom to keep them connected to the B&B. Deciding the kitchen was hers for the duration of her stay, she fetched plates, cups, napkins, and silverware as Jake and Dalton opened the numerous Chinese containers. Goldie followed Dalton, running circles around his feet in a way that made it easy to imagine how Jemma had tripped over the Goldendoodle pup.

When Jemma came in with her husband's arm around her shoulders, Bree thought she looked better for her nap. Jazz caught Trey under his arms and swung him up into his booster seat.

"Sesame chicken! I love sesame chicken!" Trey kicked his feet and leaned forward, trying to reach the container closest to him.

"Hold your horses, kid. I'll get it for you," Jazz said, reaching for a plate.

Goldie plopped beside Trey's chair, gazing up at the boy expectantly.

"No begging," Jazz said to Goldie.

The pup looked away as if guilty of being caught in the act but didn't move from her spot. Bree figured the puppy knew that Trey would eventually drop food, either on purpose or by accident.

"It's nice to have you here, Jake," Jemma said with a smile as Garth filled a plate for her.

Jake flashed a smile, making Bree's pulse jump. He was far too attractive when he wasn't scowling. "Back at you, sis."

The only empty space at the table was next to Jake. She was hungry, so she dropped beside him, then quickly helped herself to beef and broccoli over rice.

"Heard George Amos is looking to unload his boat," Dalton said as they began to eat. "Sounds like he has some financial troubles and is looking for a quick sale."

"Likely related to the way he spends all his money on beer," Jazz said wryly.

"True," Dalton agreed.

"What kind of craft is she?" Jake asked. Bree instantly knew he was considering the boat as a potential project.

"A 2005 Crownline 290." Dalton grinned. "It's a decent-sized boat, with a galley, a small dining area, and a sleeper cabin, along with a tiny bathroom, or should I say head. But I should warn you, both the interior and exterior need work. A month ago, George came to me asking how much I'd charge him to fix it up. When I gave him a quote, he quickly backed down, claiming he couldn't afford the cost."

"Price range?" Jake asked.

"A nice Crownline 290 goes for roughly fifty to sixty grand, and he's selling his for half that," Dalton said.

Bree nearly choked on her broccoli. Twenty-five to thirty grand for a boat! Talk about an extravagant purchase.

Although some would say the same for a racehorse, she supposed. Which had been far more than twenty-five grand. A long-term investment, though, with the possibility of future Rogue offspring also winning races.

"I'm interested," Jake said. "What was your quote on the repairs?"

Dalton flashed a grin. "Twenty-five grand."

"I should have known." Jake laughed, and it occurred to Bree that she hadn't heard him laugh much since they'd been in McNally Bay. He was more likely to be serious and intense, not lighthearted and fun.

A funny Jake, the way he'd been when they'd first begun dating, was doubly hard to resist.

"You can probably do it for less than half that and still make a profit," Dalton pointed out. "I've raised my prices since our little business has gotten so busy."

"And I can weasel him down in his asking price," Jake agreed. "I'll check it out, thanks for the tip."

Jazz elbowed her brother in the ribs. "Just don't think you're going to get Dalton's help with the boat, we have renovation projects coming out of our ears. We are to the point we're behind on our own stuff."

"I won't," Jake assured her. "And I can help as long as you give me relatively easy jobs to do."

"We'll gladly take you up on that offer," Dalton said.

Bree continued eating, trying not to show her disappointment. So much for Jake including her in his next project. He'd already decided on George's boat without even asking her opinion.

Not that she knew anything about boats.

Watching the interplay between Jake and his sisters, she realized he was more relaxed than she'd seen him since their arrival. Despite everything, she was glad he was willing to spend this time with his family.

It was possible that Jazz and Jemma, along with their respective husbands, could give Jake something she never could.

A place to call home.

Jake couldn't stop thinking of the Crownline 290 as a potential project and was anxious to see the craft for himself.

"Speaking of boats, we still don't know what happened to Lucy Tate." Jemma let out a sigh. "I'm so bummed. I really thought Jeremy would be able to come through for us."

Jake frowned, not understanding what his sister was talking about. "Who on earth is Lucy Tate?"

"The girl who died the night our dad took her and several of his friends out on Lake Michigan," Jazz said. "She drowned after falling overboard."

"Our dad?" He still wasn't getting it. "Was Mom on the boat, too?"

"No, silly." Jemma smiled. "We're talking about well over fifty years ago, when Dad was seventeen and Lucy was sixteen. He and Mom didn't meet until college. Didn't we show you the letter?"

"No." He felt marginally better knowing that whatever happened between his dad and Lucy was before his father had met and married their mom. His parents had been very much in love, and losing them six years ago had been hard.

The only thing that helped him get through it was knowing they'd gone to heaven together.

"I'll get it," Jazz offered. She jumped up from the table, returning a few minutes later with an old Bible. She set it in front of him and opened it to reveal a yellowed slip of paper tucked inside. "Jemma found this in the attic a few months ago, and we've been working on unraveling the mystery around Lucy's death ever since."

"What does it say?" Bree leaned over his arm as if to get a better look at the letter. Even after a long day of travel, she still smelled amazingly like an Irish breeze.

He cleared his throat and began to read out loud:

"Dearest Lucy,

My world is dark without you in it. I don't understand how this happened, and I'm finding it difficult to move on without you.

Life is so precious yet so brief. In one fleeting moment it's gone, as if it had never been. I've searched the Bible for answers but have found no solace to ease my pain. Some would say I haven't tried hard enough, and that may be true. It isn't easy to dissect one's mistakes, holding them up to the glaring light of day.

This suffering is my price to pay.

Always, J."

"Wow," Bree said on a sigh. "Terribly romantic, isn't it?"

"It's more confusing than romantic." Jake looked at his sisters. "Why are you so convinced this was written by Dad?"

"Because we already know that Dad and Lucy were dating the summer she died. And because Leon Tate, Lucy's older brother, has made it clear he blames the McNallys for his sister's death." Jemma eyes were earnest as they met his. "When Jazz first started the renovations on the B and B, Leon Tate and his daughter Mary were prime suspects related to all the vandalism we experienced. Remember how the gazebo had been damaged with a sledgehammer?"

Jazz nodded. "But it turns out they were innocent of that crime."

"And Tom Duris, Jazz's former fiancé, is in jail where he belongs," Dalton said with a deep scowl.

"And don't forget Carla's mother, Irene Templeton confirmed our dad and Lucy were together that summer," Jazz said, ignoring Dalton's comment about her former fiancé. "According to Irene, Lucy was pregnant and our dad pushed her off the boat that night because of it."

"Pregnant?" For some reason that shocked him. "Really?"

"That's the theory." Jazz shrugged. "We haven't proved anything, yet."

"I don't think Irene still believes our dad killed Lucy on purpose that night though," Jemma interjected. "Carla's mother has finally come around to tolerating the McNally family."

"Only because Carla's daughter, Cassie, is a McNally, too." Jazz grinned. "Irene dotes on her granddaughter."

Jake raised a brow, wanting to get back on track. "Why on earth would anyone believe our father would hurt a young girl? He was the nicest guy on the planet. If anything, it was our mom who had the temper."

"True." Jemma smiled. "But she didn't let her anger get too out of hand with me and Jazz, it was you boys that pushed her buttons more often than not."

Jake couldn't deny he and his three younger brothers had gotten into their fair share of trouble. His smile faded when he realized that fateful night twelve years ago had been one of those times. At least for him. If only he hadn't broken into the Bombay Pub and Grill to steal a six-pack of beer. He hadn't just broken the law that night, he experienced something far worse.

He was in the wrong place at the wrong time. And had witnessed a murder as a result of his youthful arrogance and stupidity.

"Don't worry"—Jazz patted his arm as if sensing his inner turmoil—"I think Irene only said that because she was poisoned by Leon's hatred of the family. No one really believes it's true, although we'd love a chance to prove what really happened that night."

He nodded but wasn't sure what else to say about something that transpired more than fifty years ago. Bad enough that he'd been haunted by the murder he'd witnessed twelve years ago. Since that night, he'd made it his life's goal to forget about the past, focusing only on moving forward.

No reason to start looking back now.

He turned his attention to George's boat, wondering how quickly he could get a good look at it. Likely not tonight, but maybe in the morning.

He glanced at Dalton. "Do you have contact information for George? I'd like to set up a meeting with him as soon as possible."

Dalton laughed. "The man practically lives in Bombay. He's there when they open at ten thirty in the morning until nine or ten at night. Best catch him early, though, he won't remember anything you talk about once he's downed a few beers."

Bombay. Why did it have to be Bombay? Jake felt his stomach knot and pushed his plate away, his appetite having vanished. He hadn't been to the pub in twelve years and had no desire to return.

Maybe he could find another boat. There had to be more than one for sale in the area. But even as the thought formed, he dismissed it. Finding something else would take longer to investigate, and the buyer may not be as motivated to sell as George reportedly was.

As everyone opened their fortune cookies, reading the various canned slips of paper inside, he mulled over the possibility of meeting George at his place, wherever that was, instead of meeting up with him at Bombay. The man had to live somewhere nearby, right?

Bree stood and began clearing the table, so he did the same. The way she avoided his gaze made him think she was upset with him.

Again.

"I just received an email from Jeremy, he's not going to be able to return to McNally Bay until after the wedding next weekend," Jazz announced, looking up from her phone. "That means we have to finish the plans for Autumn Fest since he's tied up."

"That doesn't give us much time." Jemma frowned. "And I was hoping he'd meet with the medical examiner to ask about Lucy's autopsy since the clerk of courts has refused to release it."

"I know, it would be good to have proof that the bruise on her temple had in fact happened pre-mortem, making it clear her death wasn't an accidental drowning. And we'd know for sure about her pregnancy, too."

Autopsy? Jake froze, reliving the words he'd overheard between the two men at the mini-mart.

"That nosy family is looking for evidence."

"They won't get it."

"You'd better hope not."

"It doesn't matter, we'll be fine as long as we keep our mouths shut."

"You have more to lose than I do."

Was it possible the evidence they'd been discussing had something to do with Lucy's autopsy? But if so, why?

What did a young girl falling or being pushed out of a boat more than fifty years ago have to do with the here and now?

5

S crubbing the kitchen helped dissipate some of her annoyance toward Jake, but not all. The moment things were set to right, she slipped away, retreating to her room.

As exhausted as she was, Bree didn't find it easy to fall asleep. The more she thought about Jake's attempt to give a relationship a try, the more she wished she'd told him to take a long walk off a short pier. Didn't need this kind of turmoil in her life, did she?

But when she awoke bright and early the following morning, she felt better about being there for Jemma. She hurried into the kitchen and began making brown bread and the other sides for the upcoming breakfast. Jemma was already there, doing her best to assist with one-handed tasks. When Jazz joined them about an hour later, she sniffed the room with appreciation.

"The cranberry and walnut muffins and lemon-poppy seed bread smells delicious."

"Thank you." Bree wiped her hands on her apron. "Three couples for breakfast?"

Jazz nodded. "Those are the guests, but don't forget we need to feed Jemma, Garth, Trey, Dalton, Jake, and the two of us."

"I won't forget." Bree tried not to dwell on Jake's plan to buy the boat, the project he'd claimed they'd do together.

Soon the meal was in full swing. Bree made eight of the full Irish and six French toast breakfasts. She and Jemma and Jazz ate theirs last, once the guests had left the dining room.

Jake lingered over his tea, eyeing her as she dug into her French toast. "Everything was amazing, Bree."

"Thanks." She tried not to let his praise go to her head.

"Everyone raved about the meals," Jemma said with a contented sigh. "I cannot thank you enough, Bree, for coming to my rescue."

"I don't mind." Bree tried to think of a way to shift the attention away from her. "Tell me more about your plans for the Autumn Fest fundraiser."

"We're holding it the last weekend of September," Jemma said. "So far we have most of the small businesses in town chipping in."

"Except for Abe Crowley." Jazz let out an annoyed snort of disgust. "He gave me a flat-out no thanks, not interested the last time I approached him."

"Who is Abe Crowley?" Jake asked.

"Owner of the McNally Bay Boat Rental," Jemma said. "I know he's seen an increase in tourism business since we opened our B and B, but he doesn't seem to care about us or the fact that Clark County needs a drug-sniffing K-9 cop."

"Does he own the boat slips, too?" Jake asked.

Bree knew he was thinking about the boat he wanted to buy from George Amos.

"Yeah." Garth nodded. "He's okay, just old and cranky."

"Not as cranky as Leon Tate," Dalton added.

"Do you think Crowley would open up to someone who isn't a McNally?" Jake asked. "Like Bree?"

Hearing him say she wasn't a McNally shouldn't bother her. After all, it was true. And they'd only dated for a total of two months, between trips to England. Yet the McNally twins had been so welcoming, she'd almost felt like a part of the family.

Almost.

She finished the last of her French toast and quickly rose to her feet. "Excuse me."

"What did I say?" Jake asked as she disappeared behind the swinging door that separated the dining area from the kitchen.

She filled the sink with soapy water and went to work, scrubbing the dishes as if she could scour Jake McNally out of her life. A more obtuse man she'd never met.

"I'm sorry." Jake's low husky voice caught her by surprise. The hinges on the door were so well oiled that she hadn't heard him come in.

"For what?" She didn't turn to look at him but continued scrubbing as if her life depended on it.

"For being a jerk." He came closer, and she caught a whiff of his musky aftershave. Ironically enough, it reminded her of spring in Ireland. "I didn't mean to upset you."

She closed her eyes for a brief moment. "You never do."

He leaned over the counter in an attempt to capture her gaze. "I've never been in a relationship like this, Bree. I'm bound to make mistakes."

She let out a sigh, pulling her hands from the sink and drying them on a towel. For some unknown reason, she had trouble staying mad at him. But she wasn't about to be a doormat either. "It's not just what you said this morning. It's how you act every day. You decided to buy a boat as your next project, one you said we'd work on together, without asking my opinion."

He grimaced and slowly nodded. "I didn't buy it yet, but you're right, I should have included you."

She tilted her head, regarding him thoughtfully. "And what do you know about boats?"

He grinned. "Nothing. But that's never stopped me before. I didn't know anything about horse racing either, until I met you."

She reluctantly smiled. "Truth be told, I still can't figure out how you've managed to find so many ways to make quid."

His grin faded, his dark eyes probing hers. "Bree, will you go with me to see George about buying his boat? It's not a done deal until we negotiate a good price."

If she was smart, she wouldn't go. Keeping her distance from Jake would be in her own best interest. Yet she couldn't summon the strength to say no. "Once the kitchen is cleaned."

"Great. Thanks." His smile seemed lighter somehow, as if knowing he'd hurt her had weighed on him in some way. "I'll do better."

"Sure you will." She turned back toward the sink to finish up the rest of the dishes while thinking that he couldn't very well do much worse.

JAKE TOLD himself the best thing he could do for Brianna was to set her free. He was lousy with relationships and had spoken without thinking.

When Jemma and Jazz had both glared at him, he hadn't understood what he'd done wrong. Jazz had smacked him on the shoulder and Jemma had kicked him beneath the table.

The truth was that he'd been alone for a very long time. Thinking about someone else, getting their advice, opinions, and even approval, did not come naturally.

Yet now that Bree had agreed to come along to his discussion with George, he felt calmer about heading over to the Bombay Pub and Grill to meet with him. Especially since it appeared no one had a clue where the guy lived. Jazz had told him to contact Jeremy because his girlfriend and soon-to-be K-9 officer, Trina Waldorf, likely knew the location, but he'd decided that might raise too many red flags.

It was well past time for him to put his old fear about McNally Bay to rest. He wasn't a scared kid any longer. The murder he'd witnessed was a long time ago.

But the two men involved were still here. And may hold a grudge against his family.

"Jake?"

Jazz's voice brought him out of his thoughts, making him realize he was standing in the middle of the dining room. "Sorry, what?"

"Are you all right?" Jazz came over and lightly clasped his arm. "You're awfully tense."

Jake figured he wouldn't really be able to relax until McNally Bay was in his rearview mirror. Which wouldn't be soon enough. "Yeah, I'm fine. Just anxious for something to do."

"Gee, I thought you'd never ask." Jazz's green eyes twinkled. "Come on, I'll show you what we're working on next door."

"Oh, but"—he glanced at the door leading to the kitchen

—"as soon as Bree is finished, we're heading over to talk to George Amos."

"I'll tell her to meet us at the house. Besides, George won't be at Bombay until they open. You've got a couple of hours to help us out, right?"

"Right." He tried to sound enthusiastic. "Let's go."

As Jazz and Dalton showed off their work, Jake couldn't help being impressed. The upstairs master suite was stunning with a beautiful view of the lake and gave him a good idea of how well the rest of the house would turn out. Dalton had a lot of design talent, and combined with his and Jazz's hard work, they were well on their way to creating something amazing.

They put him to work painting the upstairs hallway. It wasn't a lot of wall space, but his muscles were screaming in protest after an hour.

No wonder Jazz looked as if she pumped iron all day. Disconcerting to acknowledge his younger sister might have bigger biceps than he did.

The thought had him adding more elbow grease as he swiped the paint roller up and down the walls. The pale blue looked nice against the white painted wood trim.

Bree showed up just as he was finishing the last wall. "Need help?"

He wasn't about to admit how much his arms ached. "I've got it. Give me another fifteen minutes."

"Your sister and her husband are brilliant." Bree peeked into the various rooms. "Are they planning to open another Bed and Breakfast?"

"I don't think so." Although honestly, Jake wasn't sure what his sister's plans were. The house was awfully big for two people. He finished with the roller, then went to work with the brush, filling in along the taped edges of the woodwork. When he finished, he stepped back, appraising his work. "Not bad."

"It's lovely." Bree came up to stand beside him. "It's a bit like cooking a meal, standing back and appreciating the results of your work."

Jake thought it might be a little easier to cook a meal than to paint a hallway, but he wisely kept his mouth shut. "We can leave as soon as I clean up."

"Hey, nice!" Jazz came up behind them. "I wasn't expecting you to finish the entire hallway."

He gave a nonchalant shrug, glad now that he'd pushed himself to finish the task. "We're heading out as soon as I clean up the brushes and roller."

"I'll do that," Jazz offered. "Go on, I know you're anxious to find out about George's boat."

"Thanks, sis." He gave her a quick one-armed hug, then hurried into the bathroom to wash up. He made sure not to make a mess, then joined Bree. "Ready?"

She nodded, and he gestured for her to precede him down the stairs to the main level. Soon they were outside and walking through the row of trees that separated the two properties.

"Would you like to drive?" he asked as they reached the rental car.

She shook her head. "Not on your life."

"You're going to be here for at least a week or two," he reminded her. "You may want to start practicing."

"Maybe later." Bree slid into the passenger seat.

He didn't push it but took the wheel and headed down Highway ZZ toward downtown McNally Bay. He enjoyed the wooded scenery but found himself getting tense as they approached the small lakefront town. The Bombay Pub and Grill was located on the western end of Main Street. Even on a Monday, the place was crowded with tourists, and when he caught someone pulling out of a spot near the McNally Boat Rental, he quickly claimed it.

"We can walk from here, it's not far, if that's okay with you." He glanced at Bree, who nodded.

"Sure." She slid out from the passenger seat and waited on the sidewalk for him to join her. He caught and held her hand as they headed toward the pub.

Sensing her gaze on him, he glanced over. "What?"

A smile toyed with the corner of her mouth. "Enjoy being a contradiction, do you?"

"Not really. I'm trying to do better." And maybe he needed a distraction from their destination.

"How much are you willing to pay for this boat?"

"Twenty grand should do it. That gives me a good ten grand to put into renovations and repairs. If I sell it for fifty grand, I'll double my initial down payment. Not bad for an investment."

"You won't keep it?" Her expression was puzzled.

"No, what on earth would I do with a boat?" He was surprised by her question. "I don't even own a car."

"I see." She nodded, but he could tell she didn't really understand.

This was what he did. He turned things around and sold them off, before moving on to another project. Dark Rogue was his first long-term investment.

As they closed in on the restaurant, the pub looked far smaller than he remembered. As if the building had shrunk to half its size, which was, of course, impossible. The exterior of the building could have used a fresh coat of paint, but otherwise it didn't show any sign of the darkness that had taken place twelve years ago.

He didn't realize his steps had slowed to a stop until Bree tugged on his hand. "Having second thoughts?"

"Huh? Oh, no." He cleared his throat and forced himself to continue. "Just thinking that I forgot to ask what George Amos looks like."

"If he's that well known, the staff will know him." Bree gazed up at the building. "Funny, but it doesn't look like any of our pubs back home."

That made him smile. "No, it doesn't. And trust me, the Irish food isn't exactly the same either." He stepped forward and opened the door for her.

The interior of the pub was bright with sunlight, giving it a different feel from the nighttime. When his eyes adjusted, he caught a glimpse of an older man seated at the bar wearing a baseball cap and holding on to a full beer in front of him.

He instinctively knew the man was George Amos. Placing his hand in the small of Bree's back, he urged her forward. "Excuse me, Mr. Amos?"

"What?" The old man turned and squinted at him through bloodshot eyes. "Most folks around here just call me George."

"George, then." He smiled, trying to ignore the way his skin prickled as he approached the bar. "I hear you have a boat for sale. A 2005 Crownline 290?"

George's eyes widened, and he straightened on his barstool. "You interested?"

"I am, but it depends on the price."

George waved at the bartender. "Wanna drink?"

"No, thanks," Jake smiled at the disappointed bartender. He was sure the poor guy wasn't thrilled to have George as his first customer each morning. "Do you mind if I take a look at it?"

George frowned and took a long sip of his beer. "Well, she hasn't been used in a while."

His heart sank. "Does that mean the motor doesn't work?"

"It works," George quickly protested. "She just needs a little care, that's all."

He watched the older man for a long moment. "What price do you want for her?"

Again, George took another long sip as if trying to figure out how much he could make off him. "Thirty grand, and that's a bargain," he declared.

"Oh, sorry, but that's too much." Jake shrugged and spread his hands wide. "I have twenty grand saved and can't go any higher. But it's a cash offer."

George scowled. "Twenty-five," he tried again.

"Sorry, I can't do it. But really, it's fine, I'll just keep looking for something in my price range." Jake turned toward Bree. "Ready to go?"

"Sure, but I was so hoping we'd get the pretty boat." She pouted, playing it just right.

"We'll find one," he assured her. "Take care, George."

They took two steps before George called out, "Okay, you can have her for twenty. Cash only."

Jake hid a satisfied smile. He turned and walked back toward George. "I have to know the motor runs first," he cautioned. Then held out his hand. "If it does, you've got yourself a deal."

"It runs, I promise you that." George solemnly shook his hand, then reached into his pocket and pulled out a ring of keys. He pulled one off and handed it to Jake. "Try it for yourself. Abe Crowley has it in slip number eleven. And don't forget, I want cash for her."

Part of Jake was surprised the old man had given him

the key so easily. Although he suspected if he took off with the boat, Abe would call George and the Clark County Sheriff's would call the Coast Guard who would be on him like flies on raw meat. "If the boat runs, I'll return with your twenty grand in cash." He'd have to find access to his international bank accounts, but he figured Lansing would have something available.

"Great." George nodded at the bartender to fill up his beer. "I'm celebrating today, Hank."

"You celebrate almost every day, George," Hank replied dryly. "But I'm happy for you."

Jake quickly followed Bree back outside. "Let's check out our new project."

"You're a sly one, aren't you?" Bree slanted him an amused smile. "Is that how you bartered for Dark Rogue?"

"Maybe." He couldn't help but grin. "What can I say? It's one of my strengths."

"That it is."

This time, he was eager to get over to the boat rental facility. He wasn't sure how many boat slips the owner, Abe Crowley, had, but he figured it wouldn't be too difficult to find George's Crownline.

And he really, really hoped it would start. Despite the fact that he'd never owned a boat in his entire life, he suddenly wanted this one very much.

As a potential project, it was perfect. Not a huge investment that would take a long time to see a profit, but enough to give him something constructive to do.

They went around the boat rental structure to find a long pier where several boats were bobbing in the water. The slots were numbered, and when they came upon slip eleven, he drew a deep breath, trying to swallow the sting of disappointment.

The boat itself wasn't bad, but she was filthy and had lots of signs of wear and tear. "Wow, she needs a lot of work."

"She does. But that's what makes her a good deal, doesn't it?" Bree gestured to the craft. "Let's see if the motor works."

He jumped on board, then held up a hand for Bree. Taking it, she nimbly joined him. They ducked inside the small cabin area where the wear wasn't quite as noticeable.

"Looks decent," he said to Bree. "The interior needs a good cleaning but only minor repairs. I need to head up to the bridge to start the engine."

"I'm going to look around a bit more," Bree said. "I'm surprised it has space for cooking and sleeping."

"Maybe I can live here when the rooms are all booked at the B and B," he joked.

"Why not?"

The more he saw of the boat, the more he warmed to the idea of buying her. The vessel was far bigger than he'd imagined, and it occurred to him the craft would be stuck here on Lake Michigan without a trailer. Did George have one? Might be worth buying that, too.

To his surprise, the engine sputtered for only a moment, then roared to life. He wasn't a gearhead like his brother Jesse, but the motor sounded okay, no weird clicks or anything. No doubt he'd need to pay for a tune-up.

One of many things he'd need to repair or flat-out replace.

He was so preoccupied with the idea of buying the boat he didn't notice the man on the pier.

"Hey, what are you doing on George's boat?"

The familiar voice made his blood run cold. The man from the grocery store? Jake looked up as he shut the engine down.

The unshaven man from the grocery store was standing there, glaring at him.

"Hi. No need to worry, George gave me the key. I'm checking out the boat; I'm interested in buying her." He kept his tone easy as he moved out from behind the wheel. He needed to get closer to make sure his eyes weren't playing tricks on him.

"Yeah? What's your name?"

Jake hesitated, before responding, "Jake McNally. You must be Abe Crowley."

For a moment, the old man's eyes locked on his. Instantly, Jake was sent back in time to where he was hiding behind the bar at the pub.

And he knew in that moment that not only was Abe one of the men involved in the murder, but that the man had in fact seen him that night twelve years ago.

Just as he'd always suspected.

6

Bree came out from beneath the cabin, surprised to see Jake's gaze locked with that of an older unshaven man standing on the pier.

"Good day to you," she greeted the older man. "Did I hear correctly that you're Abe Crowley? Owner of the McNally Boat Rental, are you? I'm Brianna Murphy. It's grand to meet you."

Her voice caused both men to look at her as if she'd jumped out of a rabbit's hat. Had Jake forgotten she'd come along with him to see the boat? She knew he was a loner by nature, but this seemed a bit ridiculous.

Abe didn't respond but turned and walked rapidly back down the pier and back to the rental facility. She looked at Jake. "Acting a bit odd, isn't he?"

"Yeah. Odd." Jake's voice sounded weak as if he might be suffering from heat exhaustion. "Let's go."

"Seen enough?" Jake nodded and jumped out of the boat, then held out his hand to her. Her palm tingled from the impact of his touch. "Thank you." She wanted to cling to his hand, but Jake was already turning away from her, gazing after Abe Crowley.

The tension was back in his shoulders, and she didn't understand what had transpired between the two men.

"Something wrong?"

"Yeah. I mean, no." He shook his head, shrugged. "Never mind. Let's go."

"You going to buy her, are you?"

"Yes." She thought he'd be happy about his latest investment project, but a deep frown furrowed his brow. Wondering if the boat was worth the twenty thousand, was he? In cash? Quite a bit of quid.

Would he really be able to double his initial investment? Make twenty grand in profit?

She had to admit that if anyone could pull off such a feat, it was Jake. The man had a knack for making money on whatever he chose to do.

"Let's head back to the pub." Jake seemed to shake off whatever instant dislike he'd had toward Abe Crowley. "I want to pay George."

"Pay him? Carry that kind of quid around, do you?" She could hardly believe it. Where did he hide the bills? In that battered duffel bag of his?

"No, of course not." He looked at her as if she'd sprouted faery wings. "I'll need to find the closest international bank, which is likely in Lansing. Or maybe if we're lucky in Kalamazoo, which is a bit closer. Either way, I want to give George a down payment."

She nodded, feeling foolish for thinking he had twenty thousand quid stashed in his duffle. "I understand. A goodwill gesture, is it?"

"That's right." He kept his hand on the small of her back as they walked the length of the pier.

"Was Abe Crowley rude to you?"

He shrugged. "Not really. But it wouldn't matter if he was. I prefer the locals leave me alone."

Again with the sour attitude toward McNally Bay. She didn't understand why he held the town his siblings called home with such disdain. There were quite a few tourists around, but it was quaint and nice.

Not so much different than her home, well, except for the spacious green pastures and liberal amount of rain.

Still, she enjoyed the small-town atmosphere. The walk back to the pub didn't take long, and she was a little surprised when Jake handed George two one-hundred-dollar bills. "I'll bring the rest of the cash as soon as I return from the bank. Do you have a boat trailer?"

The older man's expression fell. "No trailer. Sold that off earlier this year."

It seemed odd that George had sold the trailer without the boat, but what did she know about it? Today was the first time she'd stepped foot on a private boat. The ferry between Ireland and England didn't count.

"I'll want to verify the title is clear, but if so, you've got yourself a deal." Jake held out his hand, and the older man took it.

"I don't owe anything on the boat and can get you the title." George let go of Jake's hand, drained his glass, and slid out of his seat. "Hank, don't let anyone take my spot, I'll be back soon."

"Stool has your name on it, George," Hank replied.

"No rush, I may have to drive all the way to Lansing to get the money I need from the bank." Jake walked alongside George as they headed outside.

The older man waved a hand. "I trust you. And I'll be at the pub waiting for you to return."

Bree couldn't help but smile. George reminded her of a couple of the regulars back home. Sweet and content enough to while away his time at the pub. Sure, he shouldn't be drinking so much, but at the end of the day, he was harmless.

When they reached the end of the parking lot, they split off in opposite directions. George headed toward his home, which appeared to be in walking distance of the pub, a fact she was glad for, since she didn't like the idea of him driving under the influence, while she and Jake returned to where they'd left their car parked on Main Street.

"Are we really driving to Lansing today?" Bree glanced at her phone to check the hour. "I need enough time this evening to prepare for tomorrow's breakfast."

"You drive, I'll make a few calls." Jake stopped near his rental car.

She tensed, not loving the idea of getting behind the wheel. Sure, she'd managed to make her way all the way from Kalamazoo to McNally Bay without getting lost this time, but she wasn't keen on driving around so many people. Tourists were everywhere, and she feared it would be far too easy to accidentally knock one of them off.

"Why don't you connect with the bank first? I really don't want to drive all the way to Lansing."

Jake raised a brow and peered down at his phone. He looked up with a nod and made a quick call. She overheard him talking to the bank manager, who must have been willing to give him what he needed.

"Are we set, then?"

"Yes. No need to go to Lansing, we can head for Kalamazoo instead." Jake slipped his phone into his pocket, eyeing her curiously. "Bree, the more you drive here in the US, the more comfortable you'll feel behind the wheel."

"Right you are, but not today." She reached for the passenger side door, then remembered it was really the driver's side. Skirting around the vehicle, she slid in on what would forever seem like the wrong side.

"Hungry?" Jake deftly eased out of the tight parking space without a problem. "We can stop somewhere for lunch on the way."

"I could eat something." She thought it was strange he didn't just grab a bite at the pub, but maybe knowing George was there put him off. Which was too bad since she found the older man oddly endearing. "Anywhere you like is fine with me."

"There's a great Italian place called Luccetti's located just outside Kalamazoo." He glanced over at her. "I'm sure you'll love it."

She would, but she was a little surprised he even remembered the place. Already regretting he hadn't gone to Italy, was he? Sure, he was here in McNally Bay at the moment, but for how long?

Would he even last a week?

The thought was depressing, but she forced a smile. "Sounds grand."

The drive to Kalamazoo was very different from the previous one they'd shared. Instead of being sullen and quiet, Jake talked about his plans for the boat.

"I'll need to pay someone to tune up the engine, but the rest of the repairs are more cosmetic than anything. I may need some help replacing some of the rotted woodwork. It's a shame George let her go for so long."

"Lots of cleaning, no doubt about it." She glanced at him. "I'm sure she'll sparkle when it's finished."

"I don't mind hard work."

She was a bit amazed at how content he looked over the

idea of cleaning a boat. The last time she saw him this happy was when he'd watched Dark Rogue win his first race.

It occurred to her that projects made Jake happy, but people didn't. The light didn't shine from his eyes from being near his family or staying in the town where, she'd learned from Jazz and Jemma, the McNally siblings had spent many a summer vacation.

It struck her as sad that Jake didn't find joy in the people around him.

Something she ought to remember before doing something as foolish as giving him her heart.

JAKE COULDN'T BELIEVE Abe Crowley was one of the two men he'd seen that night twelve years ago. Thinking about it made him feel sick, so he did his best to push those horrible memories away.

Focusing on his boat project helped. As strange as it sounded, he couldn't wait to get his hands dirty, cleaning and repairing the Crownline. He briefly considered naming her Lady Di, for being a diamond in the rough, then realized it would sound too much like the late Lady Diana of British royalty.

Naming her *The Brianna* would be better. But then he shook his head. Why was he picking names anyway? He wasn't planning to keep her. Still, he was looking forward to the challenge. It wouldn't be easy to get the Crownline into shape in the two weeks he'd allotted himself to stick around in McNally Bay.

Two weeks that would likely feel like two months.

"That's the restaurant you mentioned, is it?" Bree interrupted his thoughts by gesturing to a billboard. "Luccetti's?"

"Yes, that's the one." They'd made good time, and he was famished. Bree's delicious breakfast had been hours ago. "Five miles till we hit the exit."

"Why is it you Americans haven't gotten on board with the rest of the world in using the metric system?" Bree shook her head. "Like confusing the rest of us, do you?"

"Hey, I'm all for the metric system." To be fair, he'd spent equal parts of his time abroad and on US soil. "Although I'm smart enough to do the calculations in my head, so it doesn't really matter to me one way or the other."

"Go on now." She playfully pushed his shoulder, then tucked a long strand of her naturally curly dark hair behind her ear. Her blue eyes glinted with mischief. "Getting a big head, are you? I have to say, it's not a good look. I fancy a humble man, not a show-off."

"Fancy me, do you?" He mimicked her Irish accent.

"Maybe, maybe not." She tossed her hair and smiled.

In that moment, she was so beautiful she stole his breath.

This was why he'd followed her back to McNally Bay. Why he'd planned to return to Collinstown with her.

Why he hadn't been able to force himself to get on the plane to Florence.

He mentally braced for the familiar sense of panic and was surprised when it didn't come. The idea that he may have found his soul mate made him smile.

"What's your favorite Italian dish?" He took the exit advertised by the billboard, craning his neck to check the location of the restaurant. "I love lasagna, and their chef makes it almost as good as my grandmother did. My mouth is watering already."

"Spaghetti and meatballs." She leaned forward. "I see it off to the right."

They arrived at the restaurant less than five minutes later, but when they approached the door, the found it locked, a closed sign posted on the front.

"But—I don't understand. It was such a great place." He couldn't believe Luccetti's was closed, apparently for good.

"It's a business decision." She shrugged. "Happens all the time."

He scowled, hating to admit she was right, and glanced around. "Looks like there's a family restaurant up the street. I'm starving, so I guess that will have to do."

"Do you think they have spaghetti and meatballs?" Her lips quirked in a smile.

"If they do, I doubt it's nearly as good as Luccetti's." He tried to shake off the disappointment. Bree was right about the closing of the restaurant being a business decision. Either you made enough money to stay afloat or you didn't.

The fact that the restaurant was still on the billboard indicated it had closed recently.

"It's not far, let's walk," Bree suggested.

He figured it wouldn't hurt to leave their rental here at Luccetti's. They'd only taken a few steps when a large black truck with tinted windows came barreling down the road, almost as if it were heading straight for them. He instinctively pushed Bree behind him. He lifted a hand toward the driver. "Hey, watch it!"

The tinted windows made it impossible to see the face of the man behind the wheel. And the truck didn't veer off as he'd expected.

It continued straight toward them.

"Look out!" He spun away from the truck, shielding Bree

with his body the best he could. The front bumper clipped his hip, sending him flying forward.

The pavement came up to meet him with a bruising thud.

For a moment, he simply lay there, trying to understand what had happened. The loud roar of the truck engine faded as the black pickup careened out of sight.

"Bree?" His voice was hoarse, and he pushed himself upward, scanning the area.

"I'm okay." She was sitting near him. Her hand trembled as she tucked her hair behind her ear. "Drunk driver?"

"Maybe." With a wince, he stood and gazed out to where the truck was fast disappearing from view.

A drunk driver as Bree suggested?

Or someone Abe Crowley had sent?

Jake drew in a deep, ragged breath and approached Bree. "Are you sure you're okay?"

She nodded. "Were you hit? I thought I heard a thud."

He shrugged and massaged the bruise he'd likely have as a result of being hit by the black truck.

Thankfully, they weren't seriously injured, but Jake knew the outcome could have been much different. If he hadn't noticed, hadn't tried to get out of the way, his injuries could have been life-threatening.

And the more he thought about the way he and Abe Crowley had locked gazes, the more he was forced to admit the past wasn't likely to stay in the past.

Not anymore.

The fact that Abe Crowley had recognized him, and knew his name, meant he was in danger.

And not just him, but Bree and the rest of his family as well.

A wave of fury rolled over him. This was why he'd

avoided returning to McNally Bay for so long. He'd wanted to leave the past behind, to move forward with his life. Somehow, he'd instinctively known that once he'd unlocked the chest holding the secrets of the past, there'd be no walking away unscathed.

"Jake? Sure you're okay?" Bree's voice broke into his thoughts.

"Let's get something to eat." He wasn't hungry, but he needed time to think. To consider his next move.

Even though he knew it would be his word against two other long-standing members of the McNally Bay community, he knew it was time to go to the police.

Not an easy decision to make. He hadn't come forward twelve years ago, largely because he himself had been breaking the law being in the pub in the first place.

And with his troublemaker history, he didn't think he stood a chance speaking out against two adults.

But after the near miss, he knew he didn't have another option.

He could only hope and pray the authorities would choose to believe his side of the story.

7

As much as she'd enjoyed sharing a private lunch with Jake, Bree was anxious to get back to the B&B to get things ready for the following morning's breakfast. The entire trip to Kalamazoo and back to bring the twenty grand, not to mention the additional stop for lunch, had taken far longer than she'd anticipated.

Especially after being run down by a drunk driver.

She was surprised when Jake hadn't instantly reported the black truck to the police. The idiot driver had actually hit him! She was thankful that he'd done his best to protect her from harm; they'd only escaped injury because of his quick thinking.

Jake had assured her that he'd discuss the event in detail with Garth later, but she didn't think the Clark County Sheriff's Department could do anything about a crime that had taken place in Kalamazoo.

Unless Garth happened to have friends in the Kalamazoo police department.

By the time they'd returned to McNally Bay, Bree was

itching to get back into the kitchen. Yet she went along with Jake to Bombay to meet up with George.

"Next round is on me!" George exclaimed once Jake had handed over the cash.

Jake frowned. "Hey, hold on now, no reason to spend all your money in one night."

"Yes, it's supposed to last you for a while, isn't it?" Bree gave the old man's hand a squeeze. "Hank, keep him from spending it all, will you?"

"Sure thing." Hank used a wet rag to wipe down the bar. "I promise to do my best, but George doesn't listen to anyone these days. Right, George?"

"Right." George agreed, his bloodshot eyes convincing Bree he was already well on his way to being snockered. He lifted his mug of beer. "To the McNallys." He didn't wait for anyone to join in but took a deep pull of the frothy brew.

"Thanks again, George." Jake cupped her elbow with his hand and lowered his head to speak softly into her ear. "Let's get out of here."

She didn't protest when he ushered her back outside. "Poor George. What that man needs is the love of a good woman."

Jake let out a snort. "I think he's happy just the way he is."

She frowned, wondering if that was a subliminal message. Was Jake also happy the way he was? The man was driving her mad. "Listen, I'd like to head back to the B and B, if you don't mind."

He cast a longing gaze toward boat slip eleven but nodded. "Sure thing. But I plan to begin the process of cleaning her up this afternoon."

Bree knew she shouldn't have been surprised. This was

what Jake wanted, a project to keep him occupied. Or more likely, an excuse to avoid his family.

That she was supposed to be a part of his latest project was a minor detail he kept forgetting.

"I don't mind helping you with that later." She looked him in the eye. "We're supposed to work together on this, aren't we?"

"Of course." He seemed to realize he'd done it again. "I'll need your help, or I'll never get this boat turned around in the next two weeks."

Two weeks? Another subtle message. Apparently, Jake already had a project deadline and wasn't planning to stick around for long.

"Yes, well, I also have a duty to your sisters to make sure breakfast goes off without a hitch. A bit of prep time goes a long way."

"Absolutely. And I really appreciate everything you're doing for Jazz and Jemma. I don't mind dropping you off." Jake gave the boat one last glance, then opened the car door for her. "There will be plenty of work for both of us to do."

She sighed, knowing there was no point in arguing. The ride back to the B&B didn't take long. Bree expected Jake to come inside for a moment to check on Jemma and Trey, but the instant she jumped out of the car and shut her door, he gave her a wave and drove off.

Avoiding his family, for sure. With a wry shake of her head, she headed inside. The cool air was a welcome relief from the unrelenting sun. She wasn't used to the heat incessantly beating down on her. The temperature in Ireland was warmest in August, but still often turned cool, especially in the evening.

The great room and kitchen were both empty, so she poked her head through the French doors to see if anyone was inside the gazebo. She caught sight of Jemma and Garth standing there, wrapped in each other's arms.

Feeling guilty for gawking, she ducked back inside and returned to the kitchen. Sweet, they were. Newly wed and madly in love.

The image of Jemma and Garth holding and kissing each other stayed with her for a long time.

Jemma had what she'd always longed for. A man who loved her and cared about her.

A man who would be there for her in good times and less-than-good times.

She kneaded the bread dough, trying not to get lost in a wave of despair.

It wasn't jealousy so much as realizing what was missing from her own life.

No matter how much she wanted to believe otherwise, she had to admit that Jake would never be able to give her what she wanted. What she deserved. He wouldn't be the man who tenderly held his wife in his arms. Who cared about her comfort and safety above anything else.

Sweet it was for him to try, but she knew he just didn't have it in him.

And the sooner she accepted the inevitable split between them, the faster she could move on with her life.

Once Jemma's wrist was healed to the point she could manage cooking breakfast on her own, Bree wanted nothing more than to return to Ireland.

To Collinstown, the place she would always and forever call home.

～

ON HIS WAY back to town, Jake decided to make a quick detour, stopping by the sheriff's department headquarters. Ironically, the town he had vowed to avoid was now the location of his latest project. Clearly, he hadn't thought that through. He parked and headed inside the building that housed both the jail and the offices of the Clark County Sheriff's Department. "Hi. Is Deputy Garth Lewis around by chance? I'd like to talk to him."

"No, he has the day off, but he'll be in tomorrow." The dispatcher behind the desk smiled politely. "I can get another deputy here if there's something you need to discuss."

He waved a hand. "No worries, I'll check in with Garth later. Thanks anyway."

The dispatcher looked puzzled, as if she didn't understand why he would only speak to a specific deputy. Ignoring her, he hurried back outside. It would be difficult enough to talk about the events from twelve years ago to the police, no way was he going to confess his crime to a complete stranger.

Besides, it wasn't as if breaking and entering was close to the level of murder. Which only reminded him of Abe Crowley. Jake wiped his damp palms on his pants and told himself there was no reason to be worried about being down on the boat near the old man. He felt certain Crowley wouldn't try anything close to the business he owned, otherwise why follow him to Kalamazoo?

Still, he swept his gaze over the area as he approached the boat slips along the pier, searching for anything out of the ordinary.

There were scads of tourists milling about, seemingly intent on making the most of the last few weeks of summer.

Labor Day and the cooler temperatures of fall were right around the corner.

Not that he planned to be here to experience it for himself. The minute the boat was in shape, he'd put it on the market and head out of McNally Bay.

With or without Bree.

He knew he'd messed up with her once again. It seemed to be a bad habit of his. He shouldn't have made a point of asking for her help with his latest project. He was accustomed to working alone, and no matter how hard he tried to remember, he kept forgetting to include her. Each time he left her out of his plans, she looked at him with that wounded gaze that made him feel like a jerk.

The last thing he wanted to do was to hurt her.

He cared about her, and the incident with the black truck was proof of that. He'd instinctively put himself between her and harm's way, his heart squeezing painfully at the idea of her being hurt. Yet as soon as they'd returned to McNally Bay, his thoughts had been centered on all the things he wanted to accomplish with his new boat.

Without any thought of including Bree in his plans.

He was lousy at relationships and shouldn't have agreed to give it a try. Except that he wasn't ready to walk away from her yet either.

A conundrum, for sure.

He made his way down the pier and jumped onto the boat. His boat. The gentle rocking motion helped him to relax. He headed down to the small cabin area, thinking that it might be good to start cleaning in there first, since it was highly likely he'd be spending a few nights on the boat over the weekends when the B&B was full.

No reason to sleep on the floor at Jazz and Dalton's when he had a perfectly good bunk here.

He headed down to the cabin. A sour mildew odor hit hard, and it occurred to him that the sheets, pillows, and towels had to go. Bundling them up, he wrinkled his nose and carried them topside. He started a list of things he needed to replace, hoping he could get most of them in town rather than driving all the way back to Kalamazoo.

Once that was finished, he filled a bucket with soapy water and began scrubbing every surface in the sleeping area.

As he worked, he wondered if staying on the boat overnight was the smartest thing to do. What if Abe Crowley, or the other old guy he'd overheard Crowley talking to at the grocery store, came down in the dead of night to cause him harm? He never should have given out his name, but he'd been so shocked at recognizing Crowley from that horrible night, all logical thought had fled his brain.

Was there somewhere else he could moor the boat? Maybe a spot that was actually closer to the B&B? The McNallys didn't have a pier, but maybe he could pay to use someone else's pier close by.

For all he knew, Crowley wouldn't allow him to stay here either. Unless, of course, the old guy needed the money.

It would be smart to confide in Garth as soon as possible. Maybe, just maybe, his testimony alone would be enough to put the two old men behind bars for the rest of their lives.

Yeah, right. And maybe there really was a pot of gold at the end of an Irish rainbow.

His arms ached, and he had to stop for a break after he finished with the bunk. First painting Jazz's hallway that morning and now this. Spending the last few months going between England and Ireland to watch horse racing had made him soft. He hadn't done this kind of physical work since Canada.

He'd purchased an apartment home in the heart of Toronto, renovating the place over a four-week timeframe. Maybe not with quite as much talent as Jazz and Dalton possessed, but Katerina had helped with the decorating while he'd supplied the muscle. What he couldn't replace or repair himself, Katerina had helped him find local labor at a reasonable cost.

The end result had been stunning. Even he could admit how much he'd liked how the new apartment had turned out. Far better than he'd expected, that's for sure.

But not enough to live in for the rest of his life.

Once again, he felt guilty for leaving Katerina the way he had. But it wasn't all his fault. They'd shared fun times together, nothing serious or intimate. Out of the blue, she'd abruptly declared her love for him, and her desire to marry him, and to have a family with him. When he'd protested, she claimed only she could show him what true love was all about.

Talk about overwhelming. He truly cared about Katerina, but love? The familiar surge of panic had hit hard, and he'd immediately put the property on the market, sold it for a nice profit, and decided on a whim to fly to Ireland.

Where he'd met Seamus, Quinn, and Brianna Murphy. And had decided to invest in horse racing, going on to England to help purchase a racehorse named Dark Rogue.

Looking back, it was easy to see where he'd gone wrong. First, he'd moved into the cottage on the Murphys' farm, which put him in constant and close proximity to Bree during the days he spent in Ireland. Then he'd immersed himself in learning all about horses, racing, and farming, hence the frequent and extended trips to Berkshire, England.

He'd loved everything about Ireland. The relaxed and simpler way of living. Seamus and Bree had known everything about their neighbors and the others involved in the racing circuit. Their open and welcoming hospitality.

When Bree had asked him why McNally Bay didn't seem like home, he'd been tempted to admit that the only place that had ever come close to feeling like home had been Ireland.

More specifically, the Murphy Equestrian Farm.

Irritated with himself, he tossed the cleaning rag into the bucket of dirty water and stretched the kinks out of his back. Glancing around the interior of the bunk, he nodded with satisfaction. It was clean, and once he had new sheets, blankets, and towels, he could easily envision himself living there.

Temporarily.

The sound of footsteps on the pier made him tense. Crowley? He glanced around the cabin but didn't see anything he could use as a weapon. Edging into the galley, he opened drawers as silently as possible until he found a knife.

It was likely dull as a rock, but it was better than nothing. Keeping the knife at his side, the tip pointed at the floor, he eased toward the stairs leading to the upper deck.

The footsteps were louder now as the person came closer. He forced himself to breathe, but he didn't loosen his grip on the knife. Logically, he knew the person could be one of the other boat owners, or even tourists who were heading out for a sunset boat tour.

From his angle, he could see the sun was beginning to dip lower on the horizon. The hour was later than he'd real-

ized, and he was momentarily ashamed of himself for not
calling Bree, Jemma, or Jazz to ask if they needed him to
pick up something for dinner.

The footsteps stopped. For several long moments he
couldn't hear anything but the gentle, rhythmic slapping of
waves against the fiberglass hull of the boat.

"Jake? Is that you?"

Bree's voice had him releasing a pent-up breath. "Yes, I'm
down here."

The boat rocked as she jumped on board. He climbed
the steps to the upper level, then realized he still had the
knife. Turning, he quickly returned to the kitchen and
shoved it back into the drawer, before joining Bree topside.

"Avoiding me, are you?" Bree's gaze was wary.

"What? No! Why would I avoid you?" He waved at the
lower cabin. "Come on, check out the progress I made
today."

"You didn't answer my call or Jemma's." Bree's tone held
irritation as she brushed past him to head down the stairs.

With a frown, he pulled out his phone. The black screen
indicated the battery had gone dead.

"I'm sorry, I forgot to charge my phone." He followed her
down to the galley. "I was actually just getting ready to call
you and Jemma. Happy to pick up dinner for everyone.
Gino's Pizzeria has amazing food."

The way Bree avoided looking at him was an indication
of just how upset she was. He mentally kicked himself for
not noticing his phone was dead sooner.

"The cabin cleaned up nice." She nodded with approval.
"You'll need sheets and pillows for the bed if you're planning to sleep down here."

"I know. Hopefully, Jemma and Jazz will know where I
can buy them." He took a step closer to Bree. "I'm really

sorry. I know you must have been worried when I didn't answer my phone."

"You think?" Bree spun to face him, her blue eyes slashing him like ice. "Just about got hit by a drunk driver, then you act all strange about reporting it to the Garda. And then you don't bother to answer your phone. What was I supposed to think, Jake?"

He winced. "I know, I've been irresponsible and annoying. I should have thought of calling you sooner."

"Whatever." Bree turned away from him and thrust her fingers through her riot of curls. His own fingers itched to follow suit. "I think we both know this attempt to be in a relationship has been nothing but a massive failure."

Hearing her say the words out loud should have been a relief. Hadn't the same idea rippled through his mind just an hour earlier? But the thought of losing Bree, of never seeing her again, filled him with the same flash of panic he'd experienced when Katerina professed her love for him.

"No. It's me, being an idiot." He reached out to snag her hand, preventing her from heading back up to the boat deck and the pier. "Please, Bree. Just give me a chance."

"A chance?" Her laugh sounded brittle. "Used up your last chance, you have."

He tightened his grip. "Bree, please. Don't do this."

When she turned to look at him, the wounded expression in her eyes hurt him more than if she'd punched him in the gut. Which was exactly what he deserved.

"I know I should have waited for you to finish your breakfast preparations so that we could clean the boat together. I know I've made one mistake after another with you." He wanted to draw her into his arms, but he feared she was angry enough to smack him. "I care about you, Bree.

More than I've ever cared about another woman. Please give me another chance."

There was a long pause before she sighed. "I don't see the point. You can't change who you are, and I can't change who I am. It may be better to simply remain friends."

Her words stabbed deep. He pulled her closer and cupped her cheek with his hand. Her skin was like velvet, and her hair was so soft he never wanted to let go.

"Please." The word was low and hoarse. "A chance, Bree."

Her eyes melted, and he pulled her closer still, lowering his mouth to hers. He moved slowly, giving her every opportunity to pull away, but she didn't.

Instead, she stepped into his embrace, wrapped her arms around his neck, pulled him close, and kissed him back, sending his heart and his hope soaring higher than the sun dipping over the western part of the sky.

Maybe there was a chance he could make things right between them.

8

The scorching impact of Jake's kiss made Bree forget her anger and annoyance. She reveled in the warmth of his embrace, the heat of his desire. No man had ever kissed her the way Jake did.

And she was very much afraid no man could replace him either.

But all too soon, the reality of their impossible situation wiggled its way into her mind. She broke off from his embrace, breathing hard, doing her best to gather her scattered thoughts into some semblance of order.

"Bree." The way he whispered her name made her shiver. He pressed a kiss to her temple, then another below her ear, every brush of his mouth on her skin made her tingle with awareness.

"Don't." She placed her hand in the center of his chest, preventing him from kissing her again. What was she thinking, falling into his arms the way she had? "Just because there might be a bit of a spark of attraction between us doesn't make the other obstacles go away, does it?"

"A spark?" His grin was almost as lethal as his kiss.

"More like a full-blown wildfire."

She did her best not to smile because she couldn't deny he was right. Her skin was still feeling the intensity of the flames. "Whatever. It doesn't change who we are, Jake."

His brows pulled together in a frown, his expression earnest. "I'm sorry, Bree. I know I keep messing up with you, but I can do better."

She blew out a frustrated breath. It was all well and good that Jake wanted to change, but she'd learned the hard way that going into a relationship hoping your partner would change or believing him when he claimed he would change was just asking for heartache.

You either accepted the person for all that they were, strengths and weaknesses alike, or you didn't. It was as simple and as complicated as that.

Time to change the subject.

"Jemma and Jazz sent me to fetch you for dinner. Dalton already bought several large pizzas from Gino's for the group." She took a step back, needing distance. "Are you ready to go? Or is there more you want to do?"

"I'm ready." He reluctantly released her, raking his hand through his glossy chestnut hair. "But I should have been the one to buy dinner."

She shrugged and forced a smile. "Maybe next time."

Jake carried the bucket of dirty water up to the main deck, then reached over to set it on the pier. He turned and looked at her with confusion. "By the way, how did you get here?"

"I drove." She wasn't about to admit that she'd chanced hitting the locals and tourists because she'd been deeply concerned that something horrible had happened to Jake. As she'd walked up the pier, hearing nothing but silence, her fear had grown to astronomical proportions. When he'd responded so casually, she'd been so upset she'd almost walked away without bothering to talk to him.

He held out his hand, and she held it only long enough to get off the boat. "I'll see you back at the B and B."

"Yeah, sure." He jumped up onto the pier beside her, and she noticed his gaze lingered for a moment on the boat rental building.

She hesitated, then headed back down the pier. Something wasn't right there, but as usual, Jake hadn't explained what was going on in his head.

Proof that he wasn't really able to change. She'd been foolish to think otherwise.

Back in her rental, she took a moment to think about how she'd back up and pull into traffic. Driving on the opposite side of the road took intense concentration. But she managed to perform the maneuver without hitting a pedestrian.

Score one for the Irish lass.

The drive back to the B&B was uneventful, although she pulled into the parking lot with a sense of relief. Nerve-racking, it was, and she decided she would rather cook three meals a day than drive into the busy town again.

Upon entering the great room, Jemma hurried out of the kitchen to join her. "Did you find him?"

"I did, he was on the boat. Apparently let his phone battery run dead."

"That's a relief." Jemma let out a sigh. "I'm glad it wasn't anything worse."

Worse than forgetting his family and Bree? She held back a sigh. "He'll be here soon." Bree moved past Jemma into the kitchen. It was the part of the house she felt most comfortable in. "Did you save him some pizza?"

"There's an entire pizza for the two of you to share."

Garth looked up from where he was wiping liberal amounts of pizza sauce from Trey's face.

"Only because you wouldn't let me have more," Dalton protested.

"You had plenty." Jazz gave him a playful poke in the belly. She knew Jazz was teasing him, Dalton didn't have an ounce of extra weight on his lean frame, thanks to all the physical labor he did each day.

"Maybe, but I miss Jemma's desserts," Dalton lamented.

"I'll keep that in mind for tomorrow." Bree enjoyed baking, although turning on the oven in this heat seemed a bit mad. Thank goodness for air conditioning.

"Be still my heart." Dalton put his hand over the center of his chest and flashed a grin. "My favorite is chocolate cake, if you're interested, Bree."

"Why not?" Bree liked the McNally clan. She'd been impressed by the work Jazz and Dalton had done on both the Stevenson house and Jemma's apartment over the garage.

Watching the interaction between Jazz and Dalton, and Jemma and Garth, made her realize that she'd be a fool to settle for second best.

She wanted and deserved what they had.

The sound of the front door closing indicated Jake had returned home.

She caught herself short. Only this wasn't his home, was it?

Jake didn't have a place he called home.

"Sorry to make you worry about me." Jake entered the kitchen with a sheepish grin. He went over to plug his phone into the closest outlet. "My fault for letting my phone go dead."

"Guess the boat project is going well so far." Jemma's smile seemed a bit strained, and he felt bad all over again.

"It's a project for sure. I'm going to need help from Bree to get her in shape."

Bree barely glanced at him. "Sure. Happy to help."

The lack of enthusiasm in her voice was telling. He'd hoped that her kissing him was a sign that they were okay, but apparently not. Smelling the cheese and oregano from the pizza in the center of the picnic table made his mouth water and his stomach growl. "I'm starved, thanks for dinner. Tomorrow night is on me. Anything you're interested in eating, I'll pick up for all of us."

"You may regret that offer," Jazz teased. "Dig in. We saved a pizza for you and Bree to share."

He glanced at Bree. "You haven't eaten yet?"

She shook her head. "I waited for you."

He sat down on the bench seat across from her, dishing out two slices on her plate, before filling his own. He took a bite. The pizza had grown a bit cold, but he didn't mind.

"Garth, would you mind giving Trey his bath?" Jemma held her injured wrist against her torso.

"Sure thing. Let's go, champ."

"Okay." Trey didn't protest, apparently fond of playing in the tub.

"Garth?" His brother-in-law turned to look at him. Jake tried to keep his tone casual. "When you're finished with Trey's bath, I'd like to talk to you. If you don't mind."

Garth's brows levered upward. "Sounds serious."

"It is."

Jazz and Jemma exchanged looks of concern. Garth simply nodded. "Not a problem."

"I can give Trey his bath," Jazz offered.

"I need to eat first, anyway." Jake took another bite of his pizza, savoring the tangy sauce.

"I'll be back soon." Garth lifted the little boy into his arms and carried him through the house, heading to their garage apartment.

For the first time in what seemed like eons, Bree's eyes reflected her approval. "Glad you're telling him."

"You know about this, too?" Jazz let out a harrumph. "I think we need a family meeting. Jeremy is in Lansing, but I can try to find Jesse."

"No! Don't bother Jesse, the six of us are more than enough." Sheesh. He hadn't anticipated that everyone would be involved, but he realized there was no way to keep this from his sisters. And Bree didn't know all the details either.

No one did. For twelve years he'd kept his secret. Remembering the way Abe Crowley had locked gazes with him gave him the jolt he'd needed to come clean.

He ate three slices of pizza, holding back until he was convinced Bree was finished. He helped himself to more, realizing it had been a long time since he'd been so hungry.

Performing manual labor had sure worked up an appetite.

By the time Garth returned to the kitchen with Trey, he had finished his meal and had cleaned up the kitchen.

"Why don't we sit out in the gazebo?" Jemma suggested. "We'll be able to watch over Trey and Goldie."

He nodded and followed the rest of the family outside. They had several white deck chairs available, more stashed in the garage that they pulled out for weddings, and soon they were seated in a half circle overlooking Lake Michigan.

Feeling all five pairs of eyes on him, Jake swallowed and

tried to think of where to start. He decided to start with the recent events, then go back in time.

"Earlier today, Bree and I drove to Kalamazoo so I could withdraw money to buy George's boat. We stopped at Luccetti's for lunch, but found the place was closed. As we began walking toward the family restaurant down the road, a large black truck with tinted windows drove straight toward us."

Jemma gasped. "Where you hurt?"

"We jumped out of the way, but I was hit by the front bumper. We both fell, but other than scrapes and bruises, we're fine."

"Did you get a license plate number, or at least the make and model of the truck?" Garth asked.

He grimaced. "No license plate number, and I'm not a gearhead like Jesse. It was a big black pickup truck with tinted windows. Could have been a Ford, Chevy, or Dodge."

"Two-door or four-door? Short truck bed or a long one?" Garth pressed.

He glanced at Bree, wondering if her memory was better than his. "I want to say it was a four-door, with a short bed."

Bree nodded. "I agree."

"Anything else you remember about it, like a bumper sticker?"

"None that I remember. What about you, Bree?"

"No bumper sticker. Happened fast, it did."

"Why are you first telling me now?" Garth leaned forward, resting his elbows on his knees. "Why not report the hit-and-run to the Kalamazoo police?"

"That's what I wanted to know." Bree looked him directly in the eye. "More to the story, isn't there?"

"Yeah. There's more to the story." He gazed out at the

water for a long moment. "I think the hit-and-run is related to a crime I witnessed twelve years ago."

"What sort of crime?" Garth's eyes sharpened with concern.

He hesitated. "Murder."

"Murder?" Bree's horrified tone made him wince.

Jemma brought her hand up to cover her mouth, and Jazz's jaw hung slack.

"Where did this murder take place?" Garth's voice was calm as if he heard this sort of thing on a regular basis. Which, being a cop, he likely did.

"At the Bombay Pub and Grill."

"Here? In McNally Bay?" Jazz's voice came out in a squeak. "No way."

Bree didn't say anything, but her eyes were wide with fear. "The man on the pier is involved, isn't he?"

He nodded. "He's one of them, yes."

"Wait a minute, why don't you start at the beginning?" Garth glanced over to where Trey and Goldie were playing. The way the boy and his puppy were rolling around on the grass made him wonder why they'd bothered to give the kid a bath.

"Sure. The beginning." He swallowed hard. "I'd decided to go into the pub after it closed to get a six-pack of beer. When I was behind the bar, I heard men's voices."

"You were going to steal beer?" Jemma looked horrified.

He closed his eyes for a moment. "Yeah, look, I know it was stupid, okay? I was old enough to drink, but they'd refused to sell me a six-pack. Once I got inside the place, I started having second thoughts about the plan, even considered leaving a ten-dollar bill to pay for the beer, but it didn't matter. Because I wasn't alone in the bar."

"The staff often work late to clean up after closing down." Garth's was the voice of reason.

He shook his head. "I'd waited until the bartender and server had left. Was just past four thirty in the morning when I went inside. That's why I was so surprised to hear the men begin to argue. I was so afraid of getting caught and tossed in jail I didn't really pay attention to what they were saying. But then things began to escalate."

"Go on," Garth encouraged.

"I realized they were fighting over someone talking to someone else. Still hiding behind the bar, I inched over to the edge and peered around the corner. There were three men, one of them appeared to be a bit intoxicated. I didn't recognize any of them. Suddenly, one of the men lifted a gun. My heart froze in my chest, and I thought for certain he'd pull the trigger. But instead of firing the weapon, he used it to hit the drunk man on the side of his head. Poor guy went down like a rock."

Garth eyed him thoughtfully. "Makes it manslaughter or reckless homicide, not murder."

Jake lifted a hand. "Let me finish. While the one guy was lying there on the floor, the other guy was yelling about how much trouble they were going to get in. The guy with the gun didn't seem to care. Seconds later, he bent down, lifted the guy from the floor, and levered him down the basement stairs to finish the job."

A heavy, shocked silence draped the gazebo.

"Can you identify these men?" Garth finally asked.

"I recognized their voices, but only got a good look at one of them. Not the one who threw the injured man down the stairs, but the other one." He swallowed hard. "I must have made a noise because he looked directly at me. I thought for sure the gig was up and that I'd be next to be tossed down the stairs or shot, but they took off." He didn't add that he'd hid like a frightened little girl for a good twenty minutes behind the bar before he'd gotten out of there, too.

"The man on the pier." Bree's voice was a hushed whisper.

"Abe Crowley." It felt good to have a name to go with the face after all these years.

"Abe's son drives a black pickup truck." Garth's expression turned thoughtful. "I can check it out, see if there's anything on the bumper that indicates it may have been the one that hit you."

He appreciated Garth's support. "That would be great. I don't know who the other guy is though."

"Benny Maynard," Jazz said.

"Who?" Garth frowned.

Jazz waved a hand. "The men who were on the boat the night Lucy died. Don't you see? Jake has unlocked the key to Lucy's murder! Abe Crowley and Benny Maynard were on the boat with our dad the night Lucy fell overboard. Maybe they were arguing about that in the bar that night."

He thought back for a moment, trying to capture fragments of memory from that fateful night twelve years ago. "I don't recall hearing about a girl named Lucy."

"Didn't Trina mention something about her uncle Samuel Delrosa dying twelve years ago?" Jemma glanced at Jazz. "Maybe her uncle was the guy that was tossed down the stairs."

"Yes, she did. Must be that Benny Maynard is the murderer."

"Hold on." Garth raised a hand. "You have lots of very plausible theories here, but absolutely zero evidence. You can't convict someone of a crime without proof."

"Jake is an eyewitness to what happened that night." Jazz glanced at him. "Doesn't that count as evidence?"

"If we can flip Abe Crowley on his buddy, it will. Although you have to factor in that the crime happened twelve years ago and the eyewitness is first coming forward now."

Jake felt his face redden with shame. "I was young and foolish and scared, figured the police would eventually figure out what happened using DNA or something."

"I'm not blaming you, Jake. Just stating a fact." Garth rose to his feet and went over to pick up Trey. The kid was beginning to look sleepy, so he held the boy on his lap. "Would be nice to know who died that night, before we bring Crowley in."

"Trina could probably find out from her mother where her uncle died, don't you think, Jemma?" Jazz turned toward her twin. "They'd be interested in uncovering the truth."

"Not sure that will help since it sounds as if Samuel Delrosa's death was already ruled an accident," Garth pointed out. "I'm betting he was intoxicated, his body found on the bottom of the stairs. Who would doubt he'd fallen by accident?"

Jake didn't like where the conversation was going. "You're saying the hit-and-run attempt that took place once Abe Crowley learned my name is nothing more than a coincidence? That he didn't recognize me as the kid who witnessed the murder he and his buddy committed all those years ago?"

Bree reached out to lightly squeeze his arm. "Garth is thinking like the Garda, Jake. I'm sure he believes you."

"I do believe you." Garth stroked his hand down Trey's back. The kid was snuggled against his chest, and for a moment, Jake was struck by the sheer trust and innocence the little boy felt toward his stepfather. He missed his own parents, wished he hadn't kept his distance for so long. "Bree's right. Part of the job is to look at the issue from all possible angles. Once we can confirm the identity of the guy who died that night, we can begin to put the rest of the puzzle pieces into place."

"Yeah, sure." He felt let down by the fact that Garth wasn't immediately heading out to arrest Abe Crowley. "I understand you want to get it right."

"I want to build a case and get it right," Garth said. "In the meantime, you may want to keep your distance from Abe Crowley. If he or his son was the driver of the black truck, then he may decide to strike again."

"I don't like the sound of that." Jemma frowned. "Can't you do something, Garth? What about at least talking to Abe, letting him know the police are watching?"

"It would only tip him off." Garth reached out for Jemma's hand. "I'll make sure the rest of the deputies keep an eye on Jake. If he stays away from Crowley, he should be okay."

"That's not going to happen." They all stared at him in surprise. "What? I can't stay away; my boat is moored on the pier outside of his rental business."

"There must be another place to keep your boat." Bree's expression was troubled.

She had a point, but he didn't think it would be so easy. He could look for another place, but in the meantime, he wasn't going to stop working on his latest project.

But it might be smart to convince Bree she was better off not helping him. It was one thing to put himself in danger, but no way did he want her anywhere near Abe Crowley.

As much as he hated to admit it, breaking things off with Bree was likely the best way to keep her safe.

9

A more pigheaded man she'd ever met! Jake McNally cared more about his stupid boat project than he did about his own personal safety.

It was enough to drive her mad.

Seething with annoyance, she watched as he disappeared inside the B&B. Typical of him, running away like that. It's what he did best, didn't he?

As far as she could tell, he'd been running for years. From the past or from other women.

Likely both.

True, witnessing a murder would be traumatic for anyone. Especially seeing a man with a gun viciously attacking another person. She could only imagine what he'd gone through twelve years ago.

Yet he'd never said anything about it. All that time they'd spent together between England and Ireland yet nary a word. A secret he'd planned to keep forever, without realizing that the truth would fester like a thorn burrowed under the skin, constantly attempting to work its way out.

She knew he'd only brought it up now because of the hit-and-run.

The close call took on a new meaning now that she knew Abe Crowley was likely responsible. Not a drunk driver off his rocker, but a deliberate attempt to cause them harm.

This type of violence was a part of the US she hadn't planned to experience firsthand.

"What about Leon Tate?" Jazz's voice broke the silence.

"What about him?" Jemma asked.

"He was around back then, too, right? He was Lucy's older brother and has hated the McNallys since the night Lucy fell overboard and drowned." Jazz shrugged. "Why wouldn't he be one of the guys involved?"

"No, it has to be Benny Maynard. Remember we learned both he and Abe were on the boat that night with Lucy, our dad, and Samuel Delrosa. It doesn't make sense that Leon would be involved in the cover-up of his sister's murder," Jemma protested.

"Anything is possible," Jazz said stubbornly.

"Babe, I know Leon and his daughter Mary have been rude to you and your siblings." Dalton reached out to massage Jazz's shoulder. "But he wasn't the one responsible for the vandalism to the gazebo, or to any of the other events that have taken place over the past five months. Remember how Jesse thought Leon trashed his Corvette? Turned out we were wrong about that, too. It's time to let go of your grudge against the old man once and for all."

"I'm not holding a grudge." Jazz's protest came a little too quickly. "But if you think about it, who's to say that Leon wasn't trying to get information on Lucy's death when he killed Samuel Delrosa?"

"We don't know for sure the dead man is Samuel Delrosa." Garth rose to his feet, still cradling Trey against his chest. "No sense in arguing over who may or may not have been involved. This is a police matter now, and you all need to trust me to get to the bottom of it. Jemma, I'm going to put Trey to bed."

"Okay, but bring the baby monitor so we can hear him if he wakes up."

Garth nodded, indicating he'd heard his wife's request, then disappeared around the corner heading toward the front of the house.

"Bree, you need to find a way to stop Jake from working on his boat while it's docked near Abe Crowley." Jazz looked at Jemma. "Don't you agree?"

"Totally." Jemma gave a quick nod. "It's crazy for him to be there alone, like he was all afternoon, with a dead phone battery no less."

"I'm the last person Jake will listen to." The McNally twins acted as if she had a say in Jake's life, but that was far from the truth. A wave of sheer exhaustion overwhelmed her. "He'll do whatever he wants."

"He can be so darn stubborn!" Jazz blew out a breath.

"Yeah, not at all like the other McNallys." Dalton's dry response made Bree smile.

"You see it too, do you?" In that moment, she felt a bit of kinship with Dalton. "They're all alike, they are."

"Truer words have never been spoken." Dalton chuckled when Jazz scowled at him. "Hey, I love you, Jazz, but come on, even you have to admit that stubborn is the strongest McNally trait the six of you share."

"I plead the fifth," Jemma said with a grin. "Give it up, there's no way out of this one, sis."

"Maybe not, but if we work together, we should be able

to out-stubborn Jake." Jazz tapped her finger against her chin. "Which of our neighbors has a pier?"

"None that I'm aware of," Jemma said.

"I guess we should have built a pier for our place," Dalton said. "I'd do it now, but by the time we'd get it finished, it would be too late. Jake told me he doesn't plan to keep the boat longer than a week or two."

A week or two. It stung, even though she knew it was the truth. Bree thought it was sweet the way the McNallys brainstormed solutions to Jake's problem. His family cared more than he did.

How sad was that?

"I'm heading inside." She stood and took a moment to appreciate the way the sun was dipping beneath the edge of the horizon. Beautiful sunset. "Good night."

"Good night, Bree." Jemma and Jazz spoke simultaneously, then broke out into musical laughter.

Inside the B&B, the air conditioning was set at a level that made her shiver. She ignored it, knowing she wouldn't be chilled the following morning as she cooked breakfast for the remaining guests and the McNally family.

Tomorrow was Friday, and the wedding guests would begin arriving by three in the afternoon. She needed to check with Jemma about what plans she'd made for the special occasion. Would they only be serving breakfasts or other meals as well?

Both Jemma and Jazz had gotten married in the gazebo. The pictures had turned out so lovely, they'd successfully used them to advertise their gazebo wedding package.

A grand marketing ploy that kept the B&B full over many of the summer weekends.

A trickle of nervousness slid down her spine. Cooking

breakfast for the wedding wouldn't be a problem. No way to mess that up, was there?

Maybe she'd be better off staying focused on helping Jemma and Jazz with their business, leaving Jake to do whatever he wanted.

She didn't have any control over the man.

Not now, not ever.

As soon as Jemma's wrist was healed, Bree would fly back to Collinstown, Ireland, leaving Jake to figure out his next project on his own.

DESPITE HIS SORE muscles from hours of manual labor, Jake didn't sleep well. Nightmares of the past sneaked into his brain, causing him to wake up with a start, his heart pounding and sweat dampening his brow.

Too late now to wish he'd handled things differently. Maybe if he'd gone to the police twelve years ago, they'd have found the evidence they'd needed to put Abe Crowley and his gun-wielding cohort in jail.

He knew he'd disappointed his sisters and their husbands. Especially Garth.

And worse, he'd disappointed Bree.

He never should have returned to McNally Bay. It bothered him that his family thought him a coward—a stupid, selfish kid who'd run from a crime without ever coming forward about what he'd seen.

Not to mention, he'd broken the law by being inside the bar in the first place.

He thought he'd feel better once everyone knew the truth, but he didn't. Somehow, he felt worse.

Much, much worse.

With a groan he rolled out of bed, stretching his sore muscles. He considered skipping breakfast with the family. Daisy's Diner, located on Main Street, offered decent food, not as good as Jemma's or Bree's home-cooked meals, but not bad.

Yet the thought of running into Abe Crowley or any other older guy who may have been there that fateful night made him grimace.

Nope. For now, he'd tough it out downstairs. The minute he was finished eating he'd head over to continue working on his boat. The sooner he made the repairs, the sooner he could put it up for sale and move on.

As much as he wanted to be sure his family was safe, there was no denying it would be great to put McNally Bay behind him, for good.

After a shower and shave, he headed down to the dining room overlooking Lake Michigan. He expected to see guests, but he must have missed them because only Jazz and Dalton were seated at a table near the French doors.

"Hey, Jake." Jazz greeted him with a smile. "Come join us."

He took a seat, his stomach rumbling with hunger when he saw the brown bread French toast they were enjoying. "That looks great."

"It is," Dalton agreed. He took a sip of his coffee. "Good news, we have a pier for you to rent."

He tried not to sigh. His family meant well, but he wasn't used to having them constantly in his business. He forced a smile. "Oh yeah? Where?"

"Just a couple houses down from our place. A couple by the name of Erica and Kenny Tang live there. Their female Goldendoodle, Frieda, happens to be Goldie's mom. They're nice people, Garth checked them out before we agreed to take one of Frieda's puppies."

"That's a possibility," Jake agreed. He had to admit, having the boat closer to the B&B would make it easier to work on it. And to sleep there at night since he'd have to move out of the green room. "How much does she want for rent?"

"She offered half price of whatever you're paying now." Dalton shrugged. "Sounds like a bargain to me."

"To be honest, I'm not sure what I'm paying now." His gut clenched at the thought of asking Abe Crowley what he owed. Maybe he should take Garth with him when he faced off with the owner of McNally Bay Boat Rental. "But either way, it sounds like a deal. Thanks, Dalton."

His brother-in-law waved a hand. "Don't mention it. Besides, it was Garth's idea." Dalton grinned. "I'm just sharing the good news."

He couldn't help but smile. "Okay, once I finish breakfast, I'll make arrangements to move the boat to the Tang pier. You'll have to give me an address though."

"I don't have an address, but according to Garth, once you find our place, the only one with a white gazebo in the yard, you head west three houses." Dalton gestured toward the lake. "It's the first pier you'll see, long and gray in color."

Jake figured it couldn't be hard to miss. He rose to his feet. "I'm going to get some tea, do either of you need anything from the kitchen?"

"Nope, I'm good," Jazz replied.

"Me, too." Dalton took a bite of his French toast. "Hmm."

Since his stomach rumbled again, he decided to ask Bree to make him the French toast. As he entered the kitchen, he noticed Bree was by herself at the stove, her curly dark hair springing out of her ponytail.

It took every ounce of willpower not to sweep her into his arms for a kiss. Instead, he cleared his throat. "Bree?"

Startled, she dropped her spatula and swung toward him. "Jake. Scared me, you did."

"Sorry. Do you mind if I request one of your famous French toast breakfasts?"

Her cheeks were flushed, likely from the heat in the kitchen. "Of course, I don't mind. An order of French toast coming right up. Would you like rashers, too?"

In his opinion, Irish bacon was better than what they served here stateside, but he nodded as he reached for a mug. "Sure. A man can never eat too many rashers."

"Teakettle is still hot," she said as he picked through the tea packets.

"Great, thanks." He poured hot water over the black tea bag in his mug, then leaned against the counter, watching her work as he waited for the tea to steep.

After a few moments, she glanced at him. "Something you need?"

"No." He pushed away from the counter. "I'm sitting with Jazz and Dalton if you have time to join us."

She nodded without looking at him. "Grand. I'll bring your breakfast out shortly."

It occurred to him that he might be making her nervous, although he wasn't sure why. Bree had cooked for him a few times back in Ireland without a problem. But clearly their relationship had changed after their recent kiss. He wanted to say something about their relationship, how it might be better for them to go their separate ways when this interlude here in McNally Bay was over, but she was preoccupied with breakfast, so he returned to the dining room.

"Where are Jemma, Garth, and Trey?" He reclaimed the seat he'd vacated. "I expected them to be here, too."

"Garth is working today," Jazz informed him. "Jemma and Trey have already eaten. She took Trey to the pre-K program for some sort of parent orientation."

"Parent orientation? For a pre-kindergarten program?" Seemed crazy to him. "What's there to be oriented about? Kids play until their parents pick them up, end of story."

"Oh, not at all. The program is very structured." Jazz pushed her empty plate away. "Jemma and Garth think it will be good for Trey. He's been through a lot over these past few months and could use a bit of structure."

"Yeah, I guess you're right." Guilt nagged at him for not being around when his younger siblings had needed help. Sure, he'd shown up for his sister's weddings, but shamefully, that was about all the effort he'd made.

Yet at the same time, he wasn't surprised at the trouble they'd experienced here in McNally Bay. It was trouble that had made him leave twelve years ago, and only the deep love he felt for his sisters had brought him back.

So far, Jazz and Dalton weren't acting as if they were embarrassed about what he'd done. Garth had claimed he didn't blame Jake, but he'd felt for sure his law enforcement brother-in-law was hardly impressed with his actions either.

He gave himself a mental shake. No use ruminating over the past. The truth was out, and he had faith in Garth's ability to get the evidence they needed to arrest Abe Crowley and his murdering accomplice.

"Here you go." Bree came out of the kitchen a few minutes later with his breakfast. "More tea?"

"I'd love some."

She returned in another minute with the teakettle, refilling his mug.

"Thank you, Bree." He took a bite of his French toast and almost moaned out loud. "It's amazing."

She smiled. "Glad you like it. Yours is the last breakfast, the two guests that checked out today were up early, so I'll be closing down the kitchen. If you'd be so kind to wait, I'd like to go with you to work on the boat."

He hesitated only for a moment. "Sure, no problem."

Bree flashed another smile before disappearing behind the swinging door leading into the kitchen.

"Have you named her, yet?" Dalton asked.

"The boat?" He grimaced. "No. I thought about it, but it doesn't seem fair as I won't have her for long. Best to let the new owner name her."

"I guess." Dalton drained his coffee. "Just figured you'd have picked out an Irish name."

Like Brianna? He'd wanted to, but he knew a gesture like that would only send more mixed signals, so he'd decided against it. Ignoring Dalton's comment, he turned his attention to his food. The thick slices of brown bread French toast tasted incredible. And the bacon wasn't bad either.

"Time to go. We have more work to do on the house today," Jazz said as she stood. "Maybe we'll see you a bit later."

His mouth was full of food, so he could only nod in agreement.

Dalton and Jazz held hands as they left the dining room. He watched them for a moment, seized by a flash of longing.

Until now, he had never wanted what his siblings had. The standing joke over the past few months was that he and Jeremy had been the steadfast bachelors of the family. But then Jeremy met Trina, falling head over heels in love with the cute female sheriff's deputy, leaving him the sole McNally bachelor still standing.

A title he'd earned over the years. But one that now seemed lonely.

He finished his meal, lingering for a moment over his tea. Once that was gone, he carried his dirty dishes into the kitchen. Bree was just cleaning off the counter, having washed all the dishes.

"I'll do these quick," he offered.

"Don't be silly. They can wait. I have some prep to do a little later, anyway, along with making some dessert." She dried her hands on a towel. "Ready to go?"

"Yep." He followed her back through the dining room, to the great room, and out to the rental car.

She slid into the passenger seat, leaving him to take the wheel.

"I'm moving the boat today to a neighbor's pier." He glanced at Bree. "It's much closer to the B and B, which will work out nicely."

"Grand idea." Her expression mirrored relief.

The drive into town didn't take long, but he couldn't help tightening his hands on the steering wheel as he pulled into a parking space not far from the pier.

A strange sense of foreboding caught him off guard. He stared at the building with apprehension for a moment, then impatiently shook it off. "Let's go."

"When will you tell Abe Crowley your plan to leave?" Bree moved closer to his side.

"Not yet, but soon." He hoped to call the guy later, canceling the boat slip payments over the phone rather than facing him in person. "I'm anxious to get her settled in her new home."

Bree didn't say anything more, and he sensed she understood his reluctance to go inside. As they walked side by side, his fingers brushed hers. He almost took her hand in his, but she moved away, putting more space between them.

Disconcerted, he glanced at her. Bree was looking at the boat, her expression full of horror.

"What's wrong?" He turned to follow her gaze, a wave of fury hitting hard.

No! Even from here, it was easy to see the cushioned seats on the upper deck had been slashed open with a knife of some sort, the stuffing hanging out. And that was only the damage he could see.

He rushed forward, jumping onto the boat, the slashed seats looking worse close up. Stumbling down the stairs, he discovered mud smears and additional damage to the seating down below.

Someone had viciously vandalized his boat.

Another threat. One he didn't dare ignore.

10

"**I** can't believe it!" Bree followed Jake onto the boat, down into the cabin area, struggling to take in the massive amount of damage. "I don't understand. Who would do such a terrible thing?"

"Abe Crowley." Jake's voice was low and guttural. He abruptly spun around to head back topside. "I'm going to get him."

"Jake, wait!" She caught his arm, holding him back. "Going off half-cocked won't help, will it? You don't know for sure he's responsible."

"Who else could have done it?" Jake's expression was full of torment. He tried to shake off her grip, but she didn't let him go. "I'm not the scared young man he saw twelve years ago. He's not going to get away with this."

"Call Garth." She understood why Jake suspected Abe, but as Garth had pointed out last night, theories were not proof of a crime. "Get this incident filed with the police."

He looked at her for a long moment before relenting. Feeling the way his muscles relaxed beneath her fingertips, she let go. "Garth, first. But then I'm going to confront him. As the owner of the pier, he bears some responsibility."

"Maybe." She wasn't sure that was true. "Do you think he has cameras?"

Jake's brown eyes flared with hope for a moment, before he frowned. "If he does, I'm sure they won't be of any help." He shook his head. "You know as well as I do that he's either directly or indirectly responsible for this, Bree."

She couldn't disagree. Thankfully, Jake pulled out his cell phone and called Garth. After a terse conversation, he pocketed his phone. "He'll be here shortly."

"I'm glad." She turned to look at the damage. "Guess we should start cleaning up."

"Not until Garth gets here to see what's been done." Jake's jaw tensed. "This will blow up my renovation budget and push back my timeline." He sighed and raked his fingers through his hair. "I may not even break even on this project."

He sounded so dejected she wanted to throw her arms around him in a massive hug. Keeping her hands at her sides was difficult, so she turned her attention to surveying the damage more closely. She knew he was right about the dent in his budget. From what she could see, every single one of the seat cushions would need to be replaced.

She wondered if the boat had been moored elsewhere, would the vandals have found it so easy to strike.

Too late to think about that now. It was good that Jake had an alternative place to moor his boat. Clearly staying here wasn't an option.

"Jake?" Garth's voice caught her attention.

"Coming." Jake headed up the stairs to the upper deck. She followed, wanting to hear what Garth had to say.

"Not good, Jake." Garth had climbed on board the boat,

sweeping his gaze over the vandalism. "I'm glad you weren't sleeping here last night."

She sucked in a quick breath, realizing Garth was right. What would have happened if Jake had been sleeping down here when the vandal had come on board? Would he have been hurt, or worse?

It wasn't as if the man who'd done this hadn't killed before. What was stopping him, now?

"I wish I had been," Jake retorted. "I'd have caught the old man in the act and taken him down."

"Really? And if there was more than one of them?" Garth kept his tone level. "Face it, Jake, things could have ended very differently."

Jake's lips thinned, but he didn't say anything. "Does Crowley have cameras overlooking the boats?"

"I'll find out. You have to trust me to do my job, Jake." Garth slowly shook his head. "I'm sorry. He didn't miss a single seat cushion."

"No, he didn't." Jake scowled. "He hit all the cushions down in the cabin, too. But he didn't touch the bunk, which is a little odd. The door to the bunk was closed, maybe he was afraid I was sleeping down there."

Garth's gaze turned thoughtful. "Or he was interrupted from going any further by someone or something else. What time did you leave last night?"

"Six thirty in the evening, and it's nine-thirty in the morning now."

"Fifteen hours." Garth glanced back at the rental facility. "I'm sure the perp waited until it was dark."

"Four thirty in the morning," Jake murmured.

"What are you talking about?" Garth asked.

Jake shrugged. "That's the time I was inside the pub

when I saw the murder. This is obviously a message of some sort. Keep your mouth shut, or else."

"A message delivered too late," Garth reminded him. "You've already reported the incident to law enforcement. I took the time to write a report this morning, describing your account of the twelve-year-old murder. It's sitting on Sheriff Ed Donnelly's desk. I'm sure he'll have a lot of questions, and he'll want you to write your personal statement about the incident. I'm also hoping he'll have some answers about the players, considering he's been living here in McNally Bay for the past twenty years."

"That's grand, isn't it?" She looked at Jake. "He'll be able to verify that you witnessed the murder of Samuel Delrosa."

"Yeah, I guess." Jake looked around at the mess, his expression hard. "I still want to talk to Abe Crowley. I know he's the one who did this."

"How do you know it wasn't Benny Maynard or Leon Tate?" Garth's tone remained calm and reasonable.

"I thought you said Leon Tate wasn't a suspect?" Bree's head was beginning to spin with all the McNally Bay suspects. There were so many people who seemed to hate the McNallys, just like the old stories she'd read about the old feud between the Hatfields and McCoys.

No wonder Jake never felt as if this was his home.

"I don't really think so, but that doesn't mean I don't ask Leon where he was last night before I eliminate him from the suspect list." Garth turned and jumped back up on the pier. "I'll chat with Abe, see what he has to say."

Jake jumped up on the pier beside him. "I'm coming, too."

"You can't come with me to question a suspect," Garth protested.

She decided she was going with them. As if reading her

mind, Jake held out a hand to help her step up. "Are you saying Jake can't ask the owner of the boat rental about his insurance that might cover the damage?"

"Yeah, what Bree said." Jake flashed her a grateful smile. "I can ask about his insurance coverage and let him know I'm moving out of boat slip number eleven."

Garth threw up his hands in a gesture of surrender. "Let me talk to him first. After that, he's all yours."

She glanced at Jake, who nodded. "Fine with me," he agreed.

Jake captured her hand in his as they followed Garth up toward the boat rental facility. She knew it wasn't smart, but knowing Jake had to be reeling about the damage to his boat, she couldn't bring herself to pull away.

Despite their personal differences, which were massive, he didn't deserve this. She had no idea how much quid it would take to replace every single boat cushion, but she assumed it would be at least a couple thousand, maybe more.

At the entryway to the building, Garth looked back at them. "Stay outside."

Jake shook his head. "I want to hear what he has to say for himself."

Garth narrowed his gaze. "I'll tell you what I find out. Stay outside or I'll haul you down to jail for hindering my investigation."

Jake's expression grew grim, but he stopped in his tracks. "Fine. But you'd better keep me up to date."

"Stubborn McNallys," Garth muttered. He disappeared inside, and Bree edged closer, hoping to overhear part of the conversation.

"I like your style, Irish," Jake whispered as he came up to stand beside her.

"Shh." At first, she could hear the two deep male voices but couldn't quite decipher what they were saying. Then slowly, the words became clear.

"I don't know what happened to George's old boat."

"Don't you think vandalism might be bad for business?" Garth asked. "Who would want to leave their expensive boats here if they're going to become damaged?"

"This has never happened before. Probably someone carrying a grudge against the McNallys. Wouldn't be the first time someone lashed out at them."

"Do you have a grudge against Jake McNally?"

"Me? I don't even know the guy. I couldn't care less about him."

"But you just mentioned people will carry grudges against the McNallys just because of who they are." Bree smiled at the way Garth cornered Abe. "You don't have to know Jake McNally to hold a grudge against him."

"I don't give a flying fig about any of the McNallys."

"I'd like to see last night's video."

The abrupt change in the line of questioning seemed to knock Crowley off his game. "What? I don't have any video."

"But your sign advertises video surveillance as a threat deterrent." Again, she smiled at Garth's reasonable tone. "Is that false advertising?"

"Huh? Oh, no. Well, I had video, but the stupid system broke down last week, and I haven't gotten around to fixing it yet. In case you've forgotten, it's still the height of tourist season, and we've been slammed."

"Can you show me the paperwork indicating you've requested a repair?"

"Do you have a warrant?" Abe's tone was growing testy. "I don't have to hand over my personal business records without a warrant."

"I can get a warrant easily enough, and I'll have a deputy stationed here to make sure you don't destroy any evidence while I get what I need."

This time, Garth's comment was met with silence. She did a little fist pump and grinned up at Jake. "He's going down," she whispered.

Jake nodded. "I hope so."

"Fine, get your warrant and I'll give you my paperwork." Apparently, Abe had decided to call Garth's bluff. "The cameras are broken, and whether I've asked to have them repaired yet or not isn't exactly false advertising. If that's all you have, I need to get back to work."

"I'm staying until I'm relieved by a deputy." Garth wasn't giving up. "And trust me, Mr. Crowley, if I find any irregularities in your business paperwork—anything at all—don't think I won't hesitate to shut you down."

"How dare you?" Now Crowley's voice was loud enough to carry halfway down the pier. "I run an honest business, Deputy Lewis, and have for over fifty years. I took over the business from my father, and my son, Ian, will one day take over for me."

"I hope so, Mr. Crowley." The way Garth kept his cool under pressure was admirable. The Irish in her wanted to scratch Crowley's sneer from his lips.

"I think that's our cue." Jake straightened and took her hand again. "Let's go."

Gripping his hand in hers, she accompanied him inside. "Mr. Crowley? You remember me, Jake McNally?"

For a moment, a flash of horror crossed Abe Crowley's features, but then he seemed to gain a semblance of control. "Yes, you're the guy who bought George's Crownline. I just heard about the vandalism from Deputy Lewis here. I'm very sorry that happened."

She tightened her grip on Jake's hand, sensing he might snap at him.

"I'd like to get the name of your insurance carrier." Jake's smile was all teeth and didn't look the least bit friendly. "I'm planning to file a claim for the damages."

"Insurance?" Abe repeated dully. "I don't have insurance coverage for boats owned by other people. You're supposed to have your own insurance coverage."

"But my boat was in the custody of your business." The underlying note of steel in Jake's tone made Crowley flush with anger. "Therefore, I'm filing a claim against your insurance company. And if you won't give me the information voluntarily, I'll file the claim in court."

"Now wait just a gosh darn minute." Crowley's beet-red face made her fear he was a moment away from suffering a massive coronary. "Whatever happened to your boat is not my fault!"

"Oh, I think it is." Jake moved closer, his voice dropping. "I think the damage to my boat is very much your fault. So you will be hearing from my lawyer if you don't give me the information for your insurance company right now."

The two men locked gazes in a silent battle of will. Crowley abruptly turned and grabbed a pen and slip of paper. He scribbled on the note and tossed it on the counter. "Go ahead and file your claim. But you also might want to check the fine print on your lease agreement."

Jake picked up the paper and frowned. "What lease agreement?"

"Oh yeah, that's right. You didn't sign a lease agreement for boat slip number eleven, did you? George signed it. Which means you're not covered by my lease." Crowley tsk-tsked, his expression one of false disappointment. "Too bad. Better luck next time."

Jake's fingers vibrated with anger, but he didn't lose his temper. "We'll see about that, won't we? Thanks for the information. Oh, and you should know I'm pulling my boat out of here."

"Fine." Crowley smirked. "Have a good day, Mr. McNally."

She tugged on Jake's hand, drawing him back from the narrow counter that was all that separated the two men. Back outside, Jake let out a frustrated sigh.

"I never thought of the stupid lease agreement."

"I know, but it's okay. I think Garth has it covered." She wanted to reassure Jake, but she knew that it was likely he would never recoup his cost for the damage from Abe Crowley. "We'll fix her up for the same amount as before. We'll just have to find other ways of shaving costs out of the rehab budget." She flashed a grin. "We'll be creative."

The corner of Jake's mouth quirked in a smile. "You always have a sunny attitude, Bree."

"Of course." She tugged on his hand. "Let's get the boat out of here, before something else happens."

The hint of humor disappeared from his face. "Yeah. And I better find out where I can get replacements for the damaged seats. Those won't come cheap."

"I know." She felt terrible that he was experiencing the setback.

He gently tugged her close, lifting his hand to her face. "Thanks, Bree. You're the only bright spot in this project of ours."

Her heart lodged in her throat, as she hoped, prayed he'd kiss her again. But when he bent down, he simply brushed his lips across her forehead in a chaste kiss.

When he turned away, she blew her breath out in a

soundless sigh. She'd been very close to throwing herself into his arms, kissing the daylights out of him.

And she had to stifle a stab of disappointment that he'd been the one to save her from herself.

JAKE FORCED himself to step away from Brianna. He wanted nothing more than to hold her and kiss her properly, but he knew that it was better for her this way.

He led the way back to the boat, the one he'd secretly been calling *The Brianna*, intending to make good on his promise to get away from the Crowley pier.

As he helped Bree on board, he realized that the last time he'd driven a boat was twelve years ago, his last summer here in McNally Bay. It wasn't difficult to navigate in Lake Michigan, the lake was deep enough, and higher rocks were marked with bright orange buoys.

Still, he felt a sense of freedom as the boat drifted away from shore. He eased the throttle forward, going slow until he passed the no wake zone.

Then he opened her up, enjoying the wind rushing over him. Brianna was seated beside him, curls springing free from her ponytail. She gripped the edge of the boat to keep her balance but otherwise lifted her face to the sky as if enjoying the feeling of skimming over the water.

"This is brilliant!" Her voice was difficult to hear over the sounds of the engine and rushing wind. "I love it!"

He grinned, his earlier anger having faded as they left the shoreline. "Faster?"

She tucked her hair back with one hand. "If you promise not to hit anything."

"Why would I do something as silly as that?" He pushed

the throttle forward. The front hull of the boat lifted out of the water, the vessel bouncing over the choppy waves.

The fulfilling sense of exhilaration and freedom came back in a rush. He'd forgotten how much he'd once loved being on the water.

How much he'd enjoyed spending summers with his grandparents in McNally Bay.

Before he'd witnessed a brutal murder.

After a few minutes, he brought the throttle back as they approached three sailboats. Despite their reduced speed, the three boats rocked wildly in the wake he left behind.

By the time he'd brought the boat back around toward shore, most of his anger and frustration had faded away. The damage was done, by his rough estimation a solid three grand, maybe more, but there wasn't anything he could do about it.

He should have thought about getting insurance for the boat. He'd felt like an idiot for not even considering the fact that something could happen. Not that he could have planned for vandalism, but what about a boating accident of some sort? It was foolish not to consider the importance of having insurance coverage.

Normally, he didn't jump into his investment projects without thinking them through. As much as he'd like to blame Abe Crowley, he knew he bore the bulk of the responsibility.

"Is that the pier?" Bree gestured toward a long gray pier that wasn't far from the white McNally gazebo.

"That's the one." He turned the wheel of the boat in a wide circle, bringing her back around toward shore.

He pulled the throttle back, slowing their speed so he could approach the pier. "Set out the buoys," he called.

Bree dropped the buoys used to buffer the craft from the

hard edge of the pier over the sides of the boat. Then she reached out to grab one of the posts, bringing the boat in gently.

"That was so fun!" Bree's smile brightened her face. Her fresh, clean beauty never failed to make his gut clench with need.

"I'm glad you enjoyed it." He took a moment to moor the boat to the pier.

"Did your dad teach you to drive a boat?"

Her innocent question brought him up short. He hadn't thought of his parents in a while, and the hint of nostalgia was bittersweet. "Yes, as a matter of fact, he did."

As he helped Bree up onto the pier, he realized he'd forgotten about how his sisters had claimed the murder he'd witnessed was intertwined with the death of Lucy Tate.

Ironic that what had started with his father being out on a boat with Lucy well over fifty years ago may very well end with his testimony against the man his father must have once called a friend.

11

E rica Tang was a nice lady, and her Goldendoodle Frieda was sweet and calm, much less hyper than Goldie. He hoped, for Jemma's sake, that Goldie would grow out of her rambunctious state at some point to be more like her mother. He offered Erica fifty in cash to keep his boat tied to her pier for the next two weeks, and she gladly accepted the money. He'd never found out how much Abe Crowley charged for boat slip number eleven and hoped his estimation wasn't too far off the mark.

He and Bree walked along the lakeshore back to the B&B. He needed computer access to get estimates on replacing or maybe repairing, depending on the timeframe and price differences, the slashed seat cushions and for other sundry items like sheets for the bunk and towels for the head.

"Much better to be so close to the Bed and Breakfast." Bree glanced over at him, her blue eyes bright with relief. "No need to drive on the wrong side of the road."

He managed a slight smile, even though there wasn't

much to be happy about. "Yes, it's far more convenient, that's for sure."

"Safer, too." Bree's expression grew troubled. "I don't like what happened, Jake. It's too easy to imagine Abe Crowley slashing the boat cushions with a sharp knife, enjoying every moment of destruction. I'm thinking you should stay overnight with Jazz and Dalton, instead of sleeping on the boat."

He shrugged. "Nah, I doubt anyone will risk coming after me while the boat is docked on private property. Too many potential witnesses."

"Not in the middle of the night, there aren't."

He couldn't necessarily disagree, but at the same time, he wasn't about to allow anyone the chance to do more vandalism. His investment was already costing him more than it should. He made a mental note to call and arrange for insurance coverage, on the off chance the person responsible tried again.

In his gut, he believed Garth would uncover the truth about Abe Crowley and maybe even confirm the ID of the guy who'd been with Crowley that night. He agreed with his sisters that the man with the gun must have been Benny Maynard since that was the same guy who'd been there the night Lucy died, but he wished he'd gotten a better look at the gunman's face.

What was embedded in his mind were the sounds of their voices. Abe Crowley's for sure, the second one he'd have to hear again. The whispers he'd overheard at the grocery store and gas station had seemed to match his memory.

But the two men weren't whispering that night. They'd been arguing, voices escalating until they were shouting.

"Jake? Did you hear me?" Bree's voice helped push away the haunting memories of the past.

"I heard you, Bree. But I can take care of myself. I'm thinking Garth scared Abe Crowley enough that he won't try anything more."

"Hrmph." Bree wasn't happy with his decision, but he wasn't about to change his mind.

Inside the B&B they went their separate ways, Bree heading into the kitchen while he went up to the green room. Jemma loaned him a laptop, so he booted up the device and began searching for everything he needed.

Two thousand dollars later, he had new seating ordered, to be delivered the following Monday, as well as bedding and towels. Those he was able to get online with overnight delivery, which was sweet.

An hour later, he heard voices from the great room. Hoping Garth had returned with news, he set the laptop aside and headed down.

Garth was there with Jemma at his side, along with Trina Waldorf, the pretty and feisty redheaded deputy who had captured Jeremy's heart. Trina was wearing her full uniform, which made him believe this was an official visit.

"Jake, you remember Trina Waldorf from the wedding, don't you?" Garth asked.

"Of course. Nice to see you again, Trina." He'd flirted with her a bit that night as a way to make Jeremy jealous. And because he'd been missing Bree. Jake crossed over to shake her hand, then glanced between the two deputies. "What's going on?"

"My uncle Samuel Delrosa fell down a flight of stairs at Bombay Pub twelve years ago, and I'm hearing from Garth that despite what we were told by the police back then, his death was not an accident."

"I'm sorry, Trina, but no, his death was no accident." It still felt strange to be talking about all of this so freely after years of keeping the secret buried deep. "I heard him arguing with two men first, then when I peeked around the corner, I saw a man holding a gun. Instead of shooting him, the guy hit him on the head, then after he'd crumpled to the ground, he picked him up and tossed him down the stairs to the basement floor."

"And the two men involved were Benny Maynard and Abe Crowley," she pressed.

"Well, Abe Crowley for sure, but to be honest, I didn't see the gunman's face."

"The two of them were on the boat the night Lucy fell overboard," Jemma said from her position next to Garth. "It had to be Benny Maynard."

"I have some photos I'd like you to look at." Trina pulled out a sheet of paper with six men's faces on it. "I'd like you to take a long look, see if any of these men might have been there that night."

It was chilling to realize that the gunman's photograph was in the mix. He took his time, staring intently at each photograph before moving on to the next.

None of them looked at all familiar. With a sigh, he handed the photo array back to Trina. "I'm sorry. But as I said, it was dark inside the pub and the gunman wasn't facing me directly. Unfortunately, I can't identify him."

Trina's eyes flashed with disappointment, but she took the photos back with a nod. "I understand but wanted to try."

"Which one is Benny Maynard?" Jemma peered over Trina's shoulder.

"This one." She tapped her finger on the man in the middle on the bottom row.

That picture hadn't even been one of the top two that he'd considered, which made him glad he hadn't tried to guess. He glanced at Garth. "What happened with Abe Crowley?"

His brother-in-law hesitated, then nodded. "I guess you deserve to know. We found the video camera was working, but it appears the cameras were turned off last night. Abe's story now is that his son must have accidentally shut it off without his knowledge. Interestingly enough, we did find a receipt for a camera repair from a month ago, and Abe claims he'd forgotten that it had gotten fixed since then."

"He's lying." Jake glanced between Trina and Garth. "You must know he's lying. He turned off the cameras so there would be no way to know who trashed my boat."

"Yeah, well, what I believe and what I can prove are two different things, remember?" Garth shrugged. "Don't worry, I've asked the rest of the deputies to help keep an eye on him. If he decides to try anything else, we'll catch him."

Jake bit back a sharp retort. He knew the Clark County Sheriff's Department was short-staffed during the busy summer months. Garth and Trina were doing the best they could.

Especially since Trina had skin in the game, considering it was her uncle who'd been murdered that night. He had to believe that she'd do her best to help find the proof they needed to link Benny Maynard to the crime.

"Thanks anyway, Jake." Trina's smile was strained. "I appreciate hearing the truth even after all these years."

More guilt assailed him. It made him realize that by keeping quiet he'd inadvertently hurt the family members of the victim.

He felt bad, then remembered Trina's plan to train a K-9 partner. "I'd like to donate to the cause."

She looked confused. "What cause?"

"Your K-9 program. I'd like to donate some money to help train your dog."

"Stevie." She smiled. "She's a great dog, and I'm heading up to Lansing for more training tonight. I owe your sisters a lot for putting together our first McNally Bay Autumn Fest with all proceeds going to Stevie's food and training. I appreciate whatever you're willing to donate."

"The whole family is involved. Jonah is donating several paintings," Jemma told him. "And of course we're offering a weekend here at the B and B. Jazz and Dalton are donating a coupon good for painting one room of the bidder's choice." Jemma's eyes glowed. "It's so amazing how the whole town is getting into the action."

"How about I donate half the proceeds I make from the sale of George's old Crownline?" He made the offer without hesitation. Frankly, it was the least he could do. "The amount I make may not be as much as I originally planned, but whatever money I make over and above my initial investment, I'll donate half to the K-9 program."

"Oh, Jake. That's so sweet of you." Jemma's eyes misted, and she left Garth's side to throw her uninjured arm around him in a half hug. "You're a great guy, Jake."

He did his best to smile as he patted her back, thinking she was completely wrong about that. He wasn't a good guy. He should have gone to the authorities a long time ago. If only he could go back and do things differently.

But all he could do was move forward.

The old cliché of better late than never didn't make him feel one bit better.

Apparently, the vicious damage to his boat was the price he had to pay for his past sins.

BREE CAME out of the kitchen and into the great room just in time to see Jemma hugging Jake with one arm.

It warmed her heart to see Jake with his sister. For far too long, he'd kept himself isolated from his family.

"Oh, Bree, did you hear?" Jemma swiped at her damp cheeks. "Jake just offered to donate half the proceeds from the sale of his boat to Trina's K-9 program. Isn't that amazing?"

"How grand." Deep down, Bree was a bit surprised to hear that Jake was willing to part with that much quid. "Generous of you, isn't it?"

Jake looked embarrassed as he shrugged. "It's nothing."

It was more than nothing, but she didn't push the issue. "Jemma, when you have a minute, I'd like to go over the wedding menu for the weekend."

"Sure thing." Jemma went up on her tiptoes to kiss Garth. "Call when you're on your way home from work. And don't forget the parking lot will be full of our guests who begin arriving at three p.m."

"Will do," Garth promised.

Jake suddenly remembered his promise to make good on buying the next meal. "Dinner tonight is my treat. Let me know what you'd like to have."

"The rehearsal dinner for the wedding is tonight, so keep it simple," Jemma suggested.

"Lasagna from Gino's?" He wasn't sure what other options there were that would provide enough food for all of them.

"Works for me." Garth grinned. "I love Gino's lasagna and make sure you get several orders of garlic bread."

"Duly noted," Jake wryly agreed.

"We need to get back out on patrol, right, Trina?"

"Right." Trina followed Garth outside, and Bree turned to Jemma.

"What is our role during the rehearsal dinner?"

"Nothing really, other than stay out of the way." Jemma gestured with her right hand. "I always offer the dining area for their rehearsal meals, and they generally cater in the food. I sometimes offer to do it for an additional fee, but thankfully this couple wanted to do it on their own."

Bree was secretly glad to hear it. Breakfast would be enough pressure. "The same goes for the wedding dinner?"

"Absolutely. I believe the bride and groom have asked the same caterer to do both the rehearsal and wedding dinners. It's some new company by the name of Cathy's Catering that has now expanded here from Kalamazoo, thanks to our gazebo wedding packages."

Jake edged toward the curved staircase leading up to the second story, clearly disinterested and anxious to escape the topic of weddings. Because he never planned to get married himself? She knew that was part of the reason he avoided getting too emotionally involved.

"I'm all packed, Jem, so the green room is yours. I'll be down at the boat if you need me."

Bree wanted to call him back, not happy to have him heading down to stay on the boat alone, but knew full well Jake would do whatever he wanted.

No matter how she felt about it.

She told herself that his working on the boat was for a good cause. Proceeds going toward Trina's K-9 program. But when Jake clumped down the steps a few minutes later, his tattered duffel bag slung over one shoulder, she was struck by the fact that he'd be leaving her very soon.

Again, no matter how she felt about it.

Jemma must have picked up on her feelings. "Are things going better between you and Jake?"

If better meant sharing a scorching-hot kiss, then yes, they were better for the moment.

Not long-term.

She forced a smile. "You know Jake, he'll never settle down. Always looking for the next grand adventure, he is."

Jemma frowned. "I can tell he cares about you, Bree. It's just that he's got a lot going on right now. Imagine witnessing a murder! I have to tell you, it makes sense to me now that he's been on the move all these years. Try to give him a chance. I'm sure he'll come around."

She wasn't at all sure he'd come around, but this wasn't the time or place to discuss her tumultuous relationship with Jake. "Let's go through the kitchen, make sure there's nothing more I need to buy at the store before tomorrow's breakfast. And I want to get started on Dalton's chocolate cake."

They spent time reviewing the menu Jemma had originally planned, which included blueberry muffins as that was one of the bride's favorites. They also decided on chocolate zucchini bread and the two main staples of a full Irish and the brown bread French toast. Bree jotted a few notes on a list, including what she'd need for Dalton's cake. "I'll pop into town to pick up the blueberries and zucchini as you have plenty of dark chocolate. I'll also grab more eggs. Won't take but a moment."

"I can drive," Jemma protested. "I'm hiring you to cook breakfast, not run all my errands."

"Don't be silly. You need to stay here in case some of the guests decide to arrive early. I'd have no clue how to deal with that." Bree wanted to head down to the boat to ask Jake to drive her into town, but she knew she was being ridiculous. She'd made the trip on her own once before without any trouble. As Jake said, the more she practiced, the easier it would be. "I'll be back soon."

"Wait! Don't forget our credit card." Jemma pulled the small bit of plastic from her purse.

"Thanks a mil." Bree slid the card into the front pocket of her capri-style jeans and walked through the B&B to the small parking lot. Remembering what Jemma had mentioned about the guests, she thought it might be best to park her rental off on the side so it would be out of the way, providing more than enough room for the wedding party.

Despite her internal pep talk, she headed the wrong way out of the McNally driveway, forcing her to turn around at the Pine Cone Campground. The traffic was busy for a Friday, and she gripped the steering wheel tightly as she concentrated on staying on the wrong, or rather correct side of the road.

As she turned onto Main Street, she was horrified to see that the tourists had doubled in number over the past few days. They were literally everywhere, crossing the street willy-nilly without so much as looking at the cars on the road.

"No extra points for hitting one of them," she muttered to herself as she craned her neck searching for the grocery store. Finally, she saw the familiar building.

There were only a couple of open parking spots. She pulled in and had to sit for a minute before she could relax enough to loosen her white-knuckled grip on the steering wheel.

Nerve-racking. And she had yet to make the trip back to the B&B. Taking a deep breath, she pushed open the door and slid out from behind the wheel.

The grocery store was crowded, but she didn't have

many items to pick up. She'd brought a couple of reusable bags from the B&B with her, yet she noticed not everyone shopping in the store used them. Wasteful, it was. But it also wasn't her problem.

When she'd picked out the best blueberries and zucchini she could find, she added a carton of eggs, wondering if there was a farmer nearby that might provide fresh ones, and another two packages of American rashers. Finally, she added the ingredients she needed to make Dalton's cake.

As she approached the self-checkout lanes, she noticed a familiar man standing in line. "George? Is that you?"

George Amos turned to look at her, his eyes appearing more bloodshot than last time, if that was even possible. "Yeah, it's me. Why do you look so surprised?"

His cantankerous tone made her smile. "It's late in the day, normally you're at Bombay by now, aren't you?" She pulled the B&B credit card out of her pocket.

"A man's gotta eat." He turned away, and she noticed that his basket contained cans of beef stew and soup.

"What you need is a good woman to cook for you, George." She waved a hand. "That food isn't healthy at all."

He looked at her, and for the first time, there was a keen intelligence in his gaze. But then it vanished, making her wonder if she imagined it. "Don't need a woman fussing over me, telling me I drink too much."

In her opinion, he did drink too much. And again, she was a little surprised he was here at the grocery store at two in the afternoon when the townsfolk claimed he spent every day on a barstool at the pub from the time they opened until they closed.

"Do you have family around these parts?" She wondered

if George had children who would be willing to offer their father some support.

"No." His tone didn't invite additional questions. "I'm fine on my own. Why don't you just go back to the McNally mansion where you came from?"

"The McNally mansion?" She'd never heard the B&B called that before. "You mean the Bed and Breakfast? There's a wedding scheduled in the gazebo tomorrow afternoon. Should be a lovely day."

George stared at her in confusion, then turned and quickly scanned his canned goods through the self-checkout station. There was an open spot next to his, so she moved in to do the same.

He finished before she did. "Take care of yourself, George," she called after him.

He completely ignored her, shuffling faster than she'd ever seen him move toward his car. Then she noticed another older man, one leaning heavily on his cane, going over to meet with him.

She stared at the two men for a long moment. Who was the balding man using the cane? Benny Maynard? As if they sensed her gaze, they turned to look at the grocery store window.

Thinking quickly, she pulled up her phone and snapped a picture. Maybe one of the McNallys would know who he was.

And if he may be related in some way to the murder from twelve years ago.

12

"Jemma?" Bree carried the bag of groceries into the kitchen. "Jazz? Anyone around?"

"Hi." Trey came running into the room with Goldie hot on his heels. "Mommy is in the basement doing laundry. Can I have a snack?"

"Um, I'm not sure. I'll have to check with your mom first." The boy was adorable, sharing the same blond hair and dark eyes as his mother's, and she buried a twinge of jealousy over the wonderful family Jemma had.

"Mommy always lets me have am—inol crackers." Trey's wide eyes begged her to believe him. "Puleeze?"

She'd noticed the boxes of animal crackers in the pantry and figured giving him a few wouldn't hurt. As she pulled the box out and opened it, Jemma came in.

"Trey, what did I tell you about having more snacks before dinner?"

"Oops." Bree quickly folded the wax paper interior of the box to protect the crackers from going stale. "I knew I should have asked first."

"But I'm hungry." Trey's lower lip trembled. "Hungry in my tummy."

Jemma sighed and relented. "Okay, you may have three more crackers, okay?"

"Okay!" Trey looked relieved as Bree handed him three animal crackers. "Thanks, Bee."

"Bree," she corrected with a smile. "And you're welcome."

"Come on, Goldie!" Trey ran out through the dining room toward the gazebo.

"He's turning four in less than a month and growing like a weed." Jemma shook her head. "I can't wait for his pre-K program to start. He needs other kids to play with to help burn off all that energy."

"I'm sure he'll love it." Bree unpacked the items she'd purchased and tucked them into the fridge. Then she remembered the picture she'd taken on her phone. "Jemma, take a look at this photo. Do you know the man with the cane?"

Jemma peered down at the screen, then frowned. "Yep, that's the infamous Leon Tate."

"Lucy's older brother." Bree made the connection. "I didn't realize he and George were friends."

Jemma shrugged. "Same age bracket, and in a small town like this, everyone pretty much knows everyone else. At least all the locals do. Not the tourists, of course."

"Right. Locals." It wasn't so different from Ireland, was it? They depended on the tourist trade as well to keep their small businesses alive. The racetrack was always a big draw for those visiting the area. "I thought it may have been Benny Maynard."

"I don't think so. I saw a picture of Benny Maynard this afternoon, but I can't say that I've seen him around town."

Jemma grimaced. "Then again, I don't get out much. I'm really hoping that sponsoring the Autumn Fest will help introduce me to more of the local families."

"Right." Bree slid her phone back into her pocket. Silly to think that she'd caught something significant by snapping the picture of George and Leon. Of course, the two older men knew each other, and likely Abe, too. "I'll make the muffin and bread batter ahead of time so everything is ready for the morning."

"Thanks, Bree. Have I told you how much I appreciate everything you've done for us?" Jemma impulsively wrapped her uninjured arm around Bree's shoulders to give her a hug. "You're a lifesaver. My wrist feels so much better after resting it for the past couple of days. Jeremy says I need to have the MRI on Monday, but I likely won't need surgery after all."

"I'm happy to hear that." Bree returned Jemma's embrace. "And don't worry about me, I told you I don't mind. It's not a hardship to cook breakfast for your family and your guests."

"That's what you say, but trust me, tomorrow and Sunday will be a bit crazy. Obviously, I'll be here to help." Jemma moved away. "When you're finished with the batter, why don't you get Jake off his boat for a bit? Tell him I'm holding him to his promise of buying lasagna and garlic bread for dinner."

"I will as soon as I bake Dalton's cake." Bree watched as Jemma went outside to find Trey and Goldie. Mixing the batter wouldn't take long. She turned her attention to making Dalton's chocolate cake, and an hour later, she made her way down along the lakeshore.

The cool breeze coming in off Lake Michigan held a hint of fall in the air, reminding her of home. She did the mental math, Ireland was five hours ahead of McNally Bay, Michigan, as they were currently in the Eastern Time Zone.

The time was almost three in the afternoon, so she quickly placed the call. "Dad? It's Bree. How are you and Quinn doing?"

"We're fine. No need for you to worry about us. Having fun in America, are you?"

Fun? Not exactly how she would have described it, but she wasn't about to tell him that. "It's grand, the weather has been amazing. I don't think it's rained since I've been here."

"Dry as a bone, is it? Can't be good for the farmers." Trust her dad to worry about farmers and livestock. "When are ya planning to come home?"

"Soon, maybe a week or so." She'd offered to help Jemma and Jazz with Autumn Fest but realized she probably wouldn't be here that long. If Jemma was right and her wrist was healing nicely, to the point she wouldn't need surgery, Bree felt certain that her time here would be cut short.

And as much as it hurt to know she wouldn't see Jake anymore, she longed for the comfort of home.

"How is Dark Rogue? Is he racing this weekend?"

"Aye, he is." A mixture of pride and satisfaction rang in her father's voice. "I'm right pleased with his performance this season."

Thanks to Jake. It was the one thing she was truly grateful for. "Listen, Dad, I have to run, but it's been grand to hear your voice. I miss you and Quinn."

"We miss you, too, but you deserve a nice holiday." Her dad's kind tone made tears prick in her eyes. "Enjoy yourself, we'll be here when you return."

"I know and I will." She brushed the moisture away. "Love you, Dad."

"Love you, too, Bree." Her father disconnected from the line.

Bree stood for a moment, staring down at her phone. She suddenly realized she belonged in Ireland, not here in McNally Bay. Not that it wasn't a nice place to visit, but even as much as she enjoyed Jemma and Jazz, this could never be home.

Her job over the next week would be to shield her heart against falling further in love with Jake.

No more holding hands or watching the sun set over the lake.

And definitely no more kissing.

JAKE SCRUBBED until his arms ached. Despite the major backslide of the slashed cushions, he felt as if he was making progress.

The head, the galley, and the captain's deck were sparkly clean. The new sheets and towels would arrive in the morning, and that should help make it look more homey. He'd called Garth and asked for a recommendation for a boat engine mechanic and was told to call a guy named Oliver Pandal. Jake had expected Oliver to be the same age as George or Abe Crowley, but it was a younger man's voice on the other end of the line. Oliver agreed to come out to the Tang pier to check on the boat engine.

Oliver looked to be maybe a year or two older than Jake, but he didn't remember him from any previous visits. Oliver hefted his portable toolbox on board and went straight to the back of the boat. "Turn her on."

Jake cranked the key. Oliver leaned over to listen.

"Okay, shut her down." Oliver used some tools and

tinkered for a bit. Since Jake knew nothing about boat motors, or cars for that matter, he waited until the mechanic had finished.

"What do you think?" Jake crossed over as Oliver put his tools back in the box.

"Doesn't sound bad," Oliver mused. "But she probably could use a good tune-up. I have time this weekend or early next week if you want to trailer her to my shop."

Jake blew out a breath. "Yeah, well the problem is I don't have a trailer."

"No trailer?" Oliver looked appalled. "You shouldn't leave a boat in the water all winter."

"I know, and trust me, I don't plan to own this boat come winter. I'm hoping to fix her up and sell her within the next couple of weeks."

"Really?" Oliver's brow lifted. "Didn't you just buy her? And what happened to the cushions? Looks like someone took a knife to them."

"I did just buy her, and yeah, someone likely took a knife to them. I have new seating on order, will be here on Monday next week." Jake sensed Oliver was more than a little interested in the boat. "She's a nice craft, and I'm willing to negotiate a bit on the price."

"She's a beaut, but probably out of my price range." Oliver shrugged. "But I know some people who may be interested. I'd be happy to put the word out for you."

"That would be great." He hesitated, then added, "Tell me, what do you know about installing new boat seating? Any ideas?"

Oliver threw back his head and laughed. "Got in over your head on this project, hey?"

Jake nodded, hating to admit that he'd jumped into something he was ill prepared for. "Maybe. Although to my credit, I hadn't planned on replacing all the seat cushions. That was nothing but a terrible act of violence. Which brings me back to my question, any idea how to get the new seating installed?"

"I grew up around boats, so yes, I've replaced seating before. I can give you a hand, it won't be as difficult as you might think." Oliver shook Jake's hand. "And I have a boat trailer you can borrow. How about we pull her out of the water and haul her over to my shop so we can work on fixing her up?"

"I'd like that, but can we wait until Monday? I'm sleeping down below for the next two nights."

"Monday works fine." Oliver pulled a business card from his pocket, which Jake gratefully accepted. Then he picked up his toolbox. "Come down to the shop first thing."

"I will. Thanks again." Jake watched as Oliver nimbly jumped off the boat, making his way back down the pier, wondering how much this was all going to cost him. His offer to donate half the proceeds may not be very much.

Oh well, he'd take some money out of his personal account to make up the difference if needed.

"Hi, Jake." He caught sight of Bree making her way toward him. She looked beautiful, but her expression was guarded as she approached.

"Hey, how are things at the B and B?"

"They're grand. First guest arrived just as I left. Jemma and Jazz will be busy for the next hour or so." She glanced back in the direction Oliver had gone. "Who was that?"

"A mechanic Garth recommended." Jake held out his hand to help Bree on board. "Oliver Pandal is going to be a lifesaver. He's going to let me borrow his trailer to pull the boat out of the water and into his shop so we can work on her. Not only will he tune up the boat motor, but he'll help me install the new seat cushions, too."

"Sounds brilliant." The words didn't match the wariness in her eyes. "By the way, Jemma asked me to remind you about the promise of picking up lasagna and garlic bread from Gino's for dinner."

"Absolutely." Although, he was grateful for the reminder. "I'll head into town soon since it sounds like they'll be busy for a bit."

"The place is mad with tourists." Bree tucked a curl behind her ear. "You might want to place an order with Gino's ahead of time so you don't have to wait."

"You were in town?" He was impressed she'd ventured there on her own. "Good for you."

"I picked up a few things from the grocery store. I saw George there."

"Are you sure?" From what he'd heard, the guy owned the stool at Bombay all day, every day.

"I'm sure." Bree pulled out her phone, played with it for a minute, then handed it to him. "Check out the picture."

The bright sunlight caused a glare, but there was no mistaking George's droopy features. "Who is the guy with the cane?"

"You don't recognize him?"

The way she posed the question had him peering closer at the screen. The guy was stooped at the shoulders, likely from leaning on his cane as he walked. His head was mostly bald, with just a bit of white hair behind his ears. Could he have been the gunman?

"No, I don't recognize him." He handed her phone over. "Why?"

"Jemma knows him—his name is Leon Tate. He's the one they were talking about the other day, has been carrying a grudge against your family for the past fifty years, he has."

"All because he blames my dad for Lucy's death." Jake shook his head. "That's a long time to hold on to a boatload of hate."

"Very true." Bree frowned and looked down at her phone. "Looks older than his years, doesn't he? The stress is likely killing him from the inside out."

Jake shrugged off the sorrow. He didn't have the power to change how the old man felt about the McNallys. That was something Leon Tate had to do for himself.

He glanced around the boat, thinking there wasn't much he could do in the next hour to pass the time, then back at Bree. She stood far away from him as if he smelled. He sniffed his underarms. Well, maybe he did. After all, he'd worked hard all afternoon. "How about you let me borrow the bathroom in the master suite for a quick shower, then we'll head into town. There's an old ice-cream parlor there, we can have a bit of dessert before dinner."

Her lips curved in a cautious smile. "Okay, but let's go in through the back door to avoid the slew of guests checking in."

He grabbed his duffel, thinking he might have one last clean shirt in there. Before he had a chance to offer to help, Bree jumped onto the pier on her own and began walking back to the B&B. He caught up to her easily enough, frowning when she subtly moved away from him.

Had he made her upset yet again? He tried to think back. Sure, she'd made a big deal out of his not going to the boat on his own, but that didn't seem to be enough to cause this sort of reaction.

"Spoke to my dad, Dark Rogue is racing again tomorrow." She sounded a bit homesick. "Hope he wins again, although he's done more than his fair share of bringing in quid for the farm."

"You must miss your family."

She nodded but didn't say anything more.

He took his duffel and disappeared inside the master suite. He showered and changed as quickly as possible. Bree was frosting a large chocolate cake. He was touched she'd made it for Dalton.

"Ready for ice cream?" He forced himself to sound cheerful.

"Sounds delish." She stood and came down the couple of steps to meet him.

They rounded the house and the garage to the rental. He paused, glancing at her. "Would you like to drive?"

She shook her head. "I was a wreck going to the grocery store. There were so many people, and they were crossing the road without even looking."

He held out his hand. "That's fine, no worries. But I'll need the keys."

She tossed them over and then slid into the passenger seat. Bree remained quiet as they rode into town, and he could see what she meant about the tourists. The place was full of activity, and he wondered how many of the people there were planning to attend the gazebo wedding.

Brilliant marketing strategy to offer the gazebo wedding package in the first place.

There wasn't a single parking spot to be had. "Maybe we should park at Gino's. That way we can place our order and then walk down Main Street for our ice cream while we wait."

"Okay." Bree stared out her passenger side window. "Gino's looks to be pretty crowded, too."

Jake sighed. "At least there's a grassy area we can use. I'll park there."

Five minutes later, he made his way inside to place his order. The line seemed to take forever, so he texted Jemma a quick note to let her know dinner may take a bit longer than usual. After he'd placed their order, he cupped his hand beneath Bree's elbow, weaving his way through the crowd. Outside, he drew in a big breath.

"That was insanely busy. I hope the ice cream line isn't that long."

"I'm sure it will be." Bree smiled, and for the first time that afternoon he thought she actually meant it.

Threading their way down the crowded sidewalk to the ice-cream parlor was only slightly better than being crammed inside Gino's. Bree had little choice but to stay glued to his side, and for that he was grateful.

She had her purse looped over her arm, keeping it wedged between them. Someone stumbled into them from behind, sending him lurching forward. He turned, biting back a flash of annoyance.

"Hey, look out!" The shout came from a stranger.

"It wasn't me," Jake protested.

"I meant, look out for the knife." The guy gestured toward him, staring in horror.

"My purse!" Bree's voice cracked.

The handle of what appeared to be a hunting knife stuck out from her fake leather purse.

Someone had tried to stab them! A chill rippled down his arms. He raked his gaze over the area, looking for Abe Crowley or his accomplice.

But there were only dozens of unfamiliar faces surrounding them.

13

Bree couldn't seem to stop shaking, the memory of her bag being dragged down on her shoulder replaying over in her head. She knew that was the moment the knife had struck the purse.

Jake called the police, and soon a deputy by the name of Blake Hastings arrived. After taking photos of the knife handle sticking out from her purse, the deputy donned a pair of gloves and removed the hunting knife. He held it up for a long moment, the blade wicked and long with a serrated edge.

The damage it could have done to human flesh was horrifying.

"Did anyone see who did this?" Blake swept his gaze over the huddled tourists before he dropped the knife into a large evidence bag.

"It was a young kid, maybe twenty," one tourist spoke up.

"No, it was an older guy with salt-and-pepper hair," claimed another.

"I saw a young woman with blue hair wearing a leather

vest with fringes. I think she had a knife," a third person said.

"This is hopeless." Bree could see the frustration in the deputy's eyes. The so-called eyewitnesses were of no help whatsoever. Deputy Hastings turned toward Jake. "Mr. McNally, are you sure you didn't see anyone?"

"I'm sure." Jake glanced at her, his gaze questioning, and she shook her head in response.

"I didn't see anyone either. It happened so fast, the sidewalk jammed with people." She swallowed hard. "I'm not sure how he ended up hitting my purse other than it was wedged between us and everyone was being jostled by the crowds."

"Good thing or the blade may have found it's mark." Deputy Hastings shook his head. "Maybe we'll get lucky enough to obtain a set of fingerprints."

"If you do, check to see if Abe Crowley is a match." Jake's voice had a hard edge to it.

"What does Mr. Crowley have to do with this?"

"Ask my brother-in-law, Garth Lewis. He'll fill you in. Suffice it to say, Abe Crowley is on the top of my suspect list. And if you need more information, we'll be at the McNally B and B." Jake took her arm. "We need to head back to Gino's. I'm sure our food is ready."

"Fine. I'll do that." Blake Hastings moved away, and the tourists just as quickly went back to their business.

Following Jake back to Gino's, she tried to make sense of what had happened. Someone had actually tried to stab them! Had nearly succeeded. Based on the vandalism of his boat, and the near hit-and-run outside the Italian restaurant, she knew Jake was right to send the deputy to Garth for additional information.

Jake had been the target of this recent attack, all because

of the murder he'd witnessed twelve years ago. A murder that involved Abe Crowley as an accomplice.

"I'm sorry about your purse, Bree." Jake kept his arm wrapped protectively around her shoulders. "I'll buy you a new one."

"Don't be daft. The purse isn't important. Just relieved no one was hurt." The idea of Jake being stuck by a knife made her shiver.

"Are you cold?" He glanced down at her.

"Shaken up is all." She wanted very much to get away from the downtown area and the massive lot of tourists.

Jake wasn't safe alone, or in a crowd. And she very much feared he wouldn't be safe until the man who murdered Samuel Delrosa was arrested and thrown in jail once and for all.

Upon returning to Gino's, they found their order was indeed ready. Bree didn't take an easy breath until they were back at the McNally B&B.

The parking area was full of cars, and from the sounds coming from the gazebo in the front of the lake, the wedding rehearsal was in full swing.

"I'm going to park by Jazz and Dalton's place." Jake made a tight Y-turn and pulled up in Jazz and Dalton's driveway. After parking next to Jazz's big red pickup truck, they walked over between a line of trees separating the properties with the food.

Everyone was waiting for them in the kitchen, to give the wedding party and the rehearsal dinner the privacy they deserved. She thought Jake might let everyone know about their close call with the knife, but he acted as if they hadn't a care in the world. The cheesy lasagna and crispy garlic bread were delicious, and Dalton couldn't say enough good things about the chocolate cake she'd made for dessert.

"Thanks for dinner, Jake and Bree, your cake was wonderful." Jemma beamed at him from her seat across the table. "I'm full."

"Me, too," Garth added.

"Yummy." Trey's face was liberally smeared with tomato sauce mixed with smears of chocolate, crumbs littering his plate.

Jazz was sitting with her hand over her lower abdomen, her expression wary. She was the only one who hadn't finished her meal or indulged in dessert.

"Feeling ill, are you?" Bree leaned toward Jazz. "Maybe a bit too spicy?"

"Maybe." Jazz glanced at Dalton, who grinned and nodded. She smiled, despite the paleness of her skin. "It's not the food. I'm happy to announce that my nausea is because we're expecting."

"A baby?" Jemma leaped up from her seat and came running over to give Jazz a hug. "Oh, Jazz, I'm so happy for you! You and Dalton are having a baby!"

"Thanks, Jemma." Jazz hugged her sister back, then took Dalton's hand. "I only found out earlier this morning using a home pregnancy test. But I think I'm probably seven or eight weeks along. Of course, I'm sure the doctor will give me a better date. I have a feeling the baby will arrive mid-March."

"Saint Paddy's Day! Luck of the Irish." Bree beamed and hoped her envy wasn't too noticeable. She was truly happy for both Jazz and Dalton, but there was a part of her that wondered if she'd ever have a baby of her own.

Of course, might be nice to have a husband first.

"Congrats, sis." Jake raised his glass of lemonade in a toast. "*Sláinte*. To the expansion of the fifth generation of Irish!"

"Here, here." Garth raised his glass and clinked it against Jake's.

Everyone was so excited about the news of Jazz and Dalton's baby, she felt certain Jake wouldn't mention the incident on Main Street at all. But as Jazz stood to clear the table, Jake gestured at her. "Please sit down, Jazz. We need a small family meeting."

"More good news?" The way Jemma glanced expectantly at her and Jake clearly indicated she was hoping for an engagement announcement.

Nothing was further from the truth.

"I'm sorry to be a downer on this happy day, but I need to let you know that there was another attempt against me." Jake's gaze met hers, his brow furrowed with concern, before he looked away. "I want every one of you to be extra careful from now on. Especially knowing Jazz's condition."

"What happened?" Garth eyed Jake steadily.

The entire mood amongst the family instantly turned somber as if sensing the news wasn't good. Jake cleared his throat. "Bree and I were walking down Main Street to get an ice cream when someone bumped into us from behind. A hunting knife had been stuck into Bree's purse."

"A hunting knife!" Jemma's dark brown eyes grew wide. "Why on earth would anyone stick a knife in a purse?"

"I'm fairly certain the knife was intended for me, Jem." Jake's tone was gentle. "I think we were jostled by tourists on either side of us when the guy struck out with the knife, burying the blade in Bree's purse rather than in either of us."

"Oh no." Jemma put a hand over her heart. "That's terrible! Garth, tell him he needs to report this to the sheriff's department!"

"We already did," Jake assured her.

"A Deputy Hastings took our statement," Jake said. "And we suggested he speak to you, Garth, as to why we believe Abe Crowley is the man responsible."

Garth nodded and pulled his phone from his pocket. "Hastings is a new transfer in and a decent cop. I'll get in touch with him right now."

Jazz twisted in her seat to face Jake. "Why do you think the rest of us are in danger? Seems that you've been the target all along."

"I know but look how close Bree was to being stabbed. He hit her purse, which happened to be tucked between us, but the blade could have just as easily cut her." Jake glanced between his sisters. "I'm worried about the both of you. At this point, I'm afraid that striking out and hurting any McNally would be enough to satisfy this guy."

"Except, I'm an O'Brien now," Jazz said with a smile.

"And I'm a Lewis," Jemma added.

Bree understood they were trying to lighten the tone, but it was clear that Jake wasn't in the mood.

"Don't brush this off!" He blew out a frustrated breath. "I'm sorry. Just—be careful, okay? Don't take any unnecessary chances."

A heavy silence cloaked them. Bree found herself edging closer on the picnic bench to Jake's reassuring warmth.

Garth came back into the kitchen. "I filled Blake in on the details. Being a new transfer in, he doesn't have a clue about the history of the town. He's going to question Abe about his whereabouts at the time of the incident."

"Will he also get Abe Crowley's prints for a match?" Bree asked.

Garth slowly shook his head. "Unfortunately, no prints were found on the knife handle. It had been wiped clean."

No fingerprints, no eyewitness. Her shoulders slumped with despair.

This was mad! Maybe it was time to convince Jake to move on. Leaving McNally Bay may be the only way to keep him safe.

And she'd rather have Jake living far away than staying here in the center of danger.

~

JAKE FELT sick at how close Bree had gotten to being stabbed. It was one thing to be the target himself, but he really didn't like the idea that his family and friends were also in danger.

"Jake, let's talk for a moment, shall we?" Bree lightly touched his elbow.

The wedding party was wrapping up their dinner and milling around the gazebo, so they went out through the great room to take a walk down toward the Tang pier.

"Time to head to Florence, isn't it?" Bree didn't look at him as she spoke. "Sell the boat to the mechanic bloke you met earlier and move on. Safer to be abroad right now, don't you think?"

"I'm not leaving until I know the truth."

"But you were desperate to leave McNally Bay behind just a few days ago."

"That was before I knew about Trina's uncle being the victim that night, and before the hit-and-run outside of Luccetti's." He tried to hide his wounded tone. "Since then there's been vandalism and a knife attack. Do you really think I can just pack up and leave my sisters here to fend for themselves?"

"They're not alone. Jemma has Garth, and Jazz has

Dalton. Both men are more than capable of protecting their own."

"Except Jazz is pregnant." The news had not only surprised him but dredged up a strange sense of longing. He'd never even considered being in a long-term relationship, until he'd met Bree. Until he'd fallen for not just her beauty, but her warmth, her smile, her love of family.

He felt certain that she was the only one for him. Not that he deserved her.

"I know. But I'm thinking they want you to be safe."

"This is my fault, Bree." He stopped on the lakeshore, looking out at the sunset. "Don't you see? I carry the burden of this mess. For not going to the police twelve years ago, the way I should have. I witnessed a murder, the taking of a man's life, and chose to stay silent rather than risk telling the truth."

"You were young, Jake. Just turned twenty-three. Seeing a man with a gun, watching him murder a man, doesn't happen every day, does it?"

"Not a kid. Old enough to drink, vote, and know better." He couldn't keep the bitterness from his tone. If only he could go back, do the right thing by coming forward. "I was a coward."

"No. You were a frightened young man who witnessed a horrific crime." The way Bree jumped to his defense should have made him feel better, but it didn't.

"I wish I'd gotten a look at the gunman. But he was behind the post and I was too afraid to move." He kept reliving those moments he'd met Abe Crowley's gaze across the pub over and over in his mind. But it was only Abe's face he'd seen that night, not the man who'd struck Samuel Delrosa before brutally tossing him down the stairs. The horrible sound Samuel's body made when it hit the bottom of the basement stairs still made him feel sick to his stomach.

He'd done nothing to stop it. Or report it. Had only stayed hidden until Abe and his accomplice left. It wasn't until dawn that he'd crawled out from behind the bar and made it back to his grandparent's house.

And he'd made up an excuse to leave McNally Bay for good the very next day.

Returning only for Jazz and Jemma's weddings.

"Garth will find him, Jake."

"I know." If he trusted anyone, it was his brother-in-law. He'd heard how Garth had put his life on the line to save Jemma and Trey back in May. He was a good cop with great instincts, not to mention the tenacity of a bulldog.

They stood in silence for a long moment. He enjoyed the sounds of the waves lapping at the rocky shore. The activity on the lake had calmed down a bit, although there were still a few boats scattered about.

It was too early to bunk down for the night. "Should we take the boat out for a spin?"

Bree smiled. "Sure, that would be grand."

"Then let's go." He'd checked the fuel levels in the gas tank earlier and knew they should be okay to take another trip around the bay. Oddly enough, the tank had been full when he'd purchased the boat from George.

As they approached the Crownline, he considered what Bree had said. Not the part about leaving town, he wasn't making that mistake again, but her suggestion of selling the boat to Oliver Pandal.

It wasn't a bad option, especially if he could get what he'd paid for it. It had been a while since he'd chosen a lousy prospect for an investment, and after his recent successes, especially with Dark Rogue, he figured he was well overdue for a failure.

Something to think about over the weekend.

"Wait, should we ring Jemma and Jazz to tell them we're heading out?" Bree asked, putting a hand on his arm. "I'm afraid they'll worry if we don't."

"I'll call them." He pulled out his cell phone and called Jazz. "We're heading out for a ride, be back in a while."

"Okay." Her voice sounded strained.

"Are you okay?"

"Dalton is making me rest in our master suite after my first bout of morning sickness. I'll be fine."

"But it's not morning."

"The baby doesn't seem to care." Jazz's tone was tart.

"Maybe he or she doesn't like lasagna."

"I'll be fine, Jake. Just be careful, okay?"

"Not as easy to get to me while I'm in the middle of the lake, right?"

"Right. But, Jake, after the knife incident, I'd really like you to spend the night here at the house with us. If you stay on the boat, I won't be able to sleep, and all that stress isn't good for the baby."

"Yeah, blame the baby." He sighed. "Okay, fine. I'll come back to your place after we take a boat ride."

"Jemma, Garth, and Trey are hanging out here, too, at least until the rehearsal celebrations are over. Dalton has them all downstairs."

"Sounds good. Later." He disconnected from the line.

"Very smart to avoid spending the night alone on the boat," Bree said.

He didn't respond because the incident with the knife had been another close call. So far, he'd managed to escape unscathed, but he wasn't going to give Crowley an easy shot at him either.

He helped Bree get on the boat, then reminded her to unhook the buoys. He went straight for the captain's chair and started the engine. The Crownline roared to life, and he patted the dashboard.

"Good girl," he said as if the boat were alive. *The Brianna* was an amazing boat. He sighed. Good thing he'd never put the name on her formally, as it was likely Oliver would choose something different.

Knowing he only had the weekend to enjoy the boat before he turned it over to Oliver, he glanced back at Bree. "Ready?"

"All set." Bree pulled in the buoys and then pushed against the pier. He moved the throttle forward, edging away from shore.

Bree joined him in the front of the boat, and he throttled up more speed. The boat responded beautifully, moving powerfully up and over the waves.

He sure was going to miss this.

"That's far enough."

The harsh low voice sent a fission of fear down his spine. He instinctively throttled back, slowing to an idle as he turned to look over his shoulder.

He expected to see a stranger, not the familiar face of the man who'd sold him the boat. "George? What are you doing here?"

"Shut her down." George glared at him through blood-shot eyes, but the gun in his hand didn't waver. Jake turned the motor off, letting the boat drift on the waves.

"George, what are you doing?" Bree's voice betrayed her fear. "I don't understand. Are you upset you sold Jake the boat?"

"I'm upset that Jake saw me throw Sam down the stairs that night in the pub." George swayed, and Jake couldn't tell if it was because of the alcohol that must be in his system or because of the waves rocking the boat.

"You?" Jake stared at him, wishing for a flicker of recognition. But there was nothing. Even the voice didn't sound very familiar, although he realized time may have changed his tone. "What about Benny Maynard? I thought Benny was on the boat that night with my dad and Lucy."

"Benny wasn't on the boat. That was a lie Abe and I cooked up between us. It was me that night. Sam knew about what happened because Abe spilled his guts. Sam demanded I tell the truth about what happened to Lucy, but I wasn't going to jail over that cheater. She was supposed to be with me, not Justin. I loved Lucy, and she was supposed to love me back."

Jake knew he had to keep the old man talking. Surely someone would notice the boat drifting on the lake without moving and call it in. Over George's shoulder he could see they were directly in line with the Jazz and Dalton's place.

"What happened that night on the boat with Lucy?" He kept his tone as nonthreatening as possible. "Why did you get so upset?"

"Lucy said we were through! That she didn't want to be with me anymore. I was so mad—but I didn't mean to hit her. It just happened." George's voice turned whiney. "It wasn't my fault she lost her footing and fell overboard. I loved her! I would never hurt her!"

But George *had* hurt Lucy. Then she'd died. "I thought my dad and Lucy were together. At least, that's the way his letter to Lucy sounded."

"Letter?" George's bloodshot eyes flashed with a hint of fear. "What letter?"

"Jemma found a handwritten letter from my dad to Lucy, describing how upset he was after her death." He glanced at the shoreline, wishing it was closer. "I'm sorry, George, but the letter proves how much my dad loved Lucy and how much she cared about him, too."

"She loved me! She was having my baby!" George screamed at the top of his lungs, but they were too far from shore for anyone to hear. For a fraction of a second, the gun in George's hand dropped down, the muzzle pointing down to the floor of the boat.

It was now or never. He pulled the key out of the ignition and grabbed Bree's hand. "Jump!"

"No!" George's cry echoed behind them, but he ignored it. The sound of a gunshot echoed seconds before he and Bree disappeared into the water, the icy coldness stealing his breath.

For long seconds, he couldn't hear anything. The water was so cold it was difficult to move. To swim. He kicked his feet, once, twice, lungs burning as he struggled to find his way up to the air.

He finally broke through the surface, gasping and searching frantically for Bree. There! She was an arm's length away, and he reached out for her.

"Swim!" His voice was hoarse, and she looked at him as if she couldn't move. "Swim, Bree. Come on." He desperately needed to get far away from George and his gun.

She tried her best, but he had to pull her along with him. If they couldn't find a way to make it to shore, they'd die.

Just like Lucy.

14

Bree's arms and legs felt like thousand-kilo weights pulling her down. She'd lost her shoes, but her water-logged clothes hung heavy on her frame. The water was so cold she couldn't move, couldn't breathe. She thought of her father and Quinn, even Dark Rogue.

In her mind's eye, she could easily picture the green hills and valleys of Ireland. Would she ever see her home, her family, again?

"Come on, Bree. Swim with me. We can do it."

Jake's voice sounded far away as if he were standing at the end of a long tunnel. They managed to get away from the boat, but the rocky shore was so distant, seemingly impossible to reach.

They were going to die here in the fresh water of Lake Michigan. Either by drowning or by George shooting them.

She braced for the sound of gunfire, but the night remained eerily silent.

"Come on, Bree. We can do it." Jake's voice buzzed like a gnat. She wanted to swat it away, to make him leave her alone. The coldness had turned into a welcome numb feeling, and she thought she could fall asleep and simply float away into the distance.

Would she see her mother in heaven? The idea made her smile.

"Bree, turn over on your back." Jake's hands pushed her until she complied.

"Go. Without me." She knew that if Jake were able to swim on his own, he'd make it out of there. Her inability to move was only holding him back.

"I'm not leaving you. Come on, kick your legs. Help me out. We can do this. Kick. *Kick!*"

She tried to do as he asked but knew her legs moved in slow motion. Certainly not with enough force to propel her forward.

Then she heard the distinctive chugging engine of a boat. "No! George! He's coming for us!" Spurred by fear, she kicked again, gaining some momentum.

Jake didn't answer but kept doing the sidestroke, dragging her along with him. But they weren't heading toward shore now but toward the boat.

No! George had a gun! He'd kill them!

The thought of being shot spurred her into scissoring her legs with more force. Pushing through the lethargy that held her back.

"Bree, it's the Coast Guard!" Jake's voice rose with excitement. "They're coming for us, Bree. They're coming!"

"W—what about G-george?" Her mouth didn't seem to be working properly.

"Don't worry about George. I took the keys to the boat. He can't get away, he's adrift on the water behind us. Maybe seeing the Coast Guard scared him. Look, they're here." He lifted his arm and waved frantically.

The motor slowed, but the hull still cut across the water

toward them. A round life preserver landed with a plop next to Jake.

"Hook your arm through this, Bree." He helped loop the life preserver over her shoulder. "She's ready! Pull her in!"

"Wait. Come with me." Bree didn't want to leave Jake behind.

But then a second life preserver landed nearby. It took her befuddled brain a moment to understand there was one for each of them.

The next several minutes were nothing but a blur. Strong arms lifted her out of the water, then set about stripping off her clothes and wrapping her in a blanket. She didn't even care that she wore nothing but her bra and panties underneath the blanket. The warmth of the fabric tucked around her felt like heaven.

She glanced up at the sky, realizing that she wasn't going to see her mother just yet. But maybe that was okay.

She was alive and would take comfort in seeing her dad and Quinn soon enough.

Her teeth began to chatter, which she thought was odd. She was warm now, wasn't she? But it seemed her body was slowly coming back to life. Her muscles jerked as she continued to shiver.

"Bree? Are you okay?" Jake's brown hair was plastered to his skull, his brown eyes full of fear as he crouched down beside her. She was glad to see he was wrapped in a blanket, too.

"I—I'm fine. Th-thanks to you." She pulled her hand from beneath the blanket to cup his face. "You s-aved my l-ife, Jake."

"We saved each other, Bree." He lifted her hand and pressed his lips to her palm in a sweet gesture. "I don't think I could have done it without you."

Not true. He'd been strong enough and determined enough to save himself, but she didn't argue. "Did you t-ell them about George?"

His gaze clouded. "Yeah. They're sending another Coast Guard clipper out to grab him. I can't believe it, Bree. All this time we thought Abe's accomplice was Benny Maynard. Never in a million years did I consider George to be a suspect."

She hadn't either and felt sick at the way she'd felt fondly toward him, thinking he was similar to the pubgoers back home.

"Over now, isn't it?" The intense shivering faded. She gently tugged her hand from his, pulling the blanket close. "Garth will toss him in jail, and Trina will have justice for her uncle."

"I still don't understand how George managed to come after me." Jake glanced over at the boat bobbing in the distance. "I would have thought he'd be too drunk to do much of anything."

"That's why we never suspected him. He had us all played for a fool."

Jake sat next to her. "I'm glad it's over."

She summoned a smile. "Me, too."

The boat gained momentum as the Coast Guard headed back to shore.

The next hour was spent at the sheriff's department headquarters. Still wrapped in blankets and holding mugs of hot tea, they were taken into different rooms and asked to provide their statements.

Garth came in to interview her, and she was right glad to see a familiar face. "Are you sure you're okay, Bree? By the way, Jemma sent me with fresh clothes for you and Jake."

"Thanks a mil." She was relieved she wouldn't be going back to the B&B in her knickers.

"Can you tell me what happened?" Garth had a notepad in front of him and looked at her expectantly.

She explained about how George Amos must have hidden below deck on the boat, waiting until they were away from shore before coming up to confront them with a gun. "He admitted to tossing Sam down the basement stairs because Sam wanted George to turn himself in over Lucy's death. Then George claimed Lucy's death was an accident but admitted to hitting her that night."

Garth scribbled notes as she spoke. "What else did he say?"

"That Lucy should have loved him because he was the baby's father."

"Really?" Garth looked surprised. "We always assumed Justin was the father."

"Logical, isn't it? But the betrayal of Lucy choosing Justin over him was too much for George. He hit her, and she fell overboard."

"George Amos is responsible for two deaths." Garth's tone was quiet. "Lucy and Samuel."

She nodded and sipped her tea. "Appears that way, doesn't it?"

"Did he admit to the other assaults against Jake? The hit-and-run, boat damage, and knife attack?"

"No. We jumped overboard before we could ask."

"I understand." Garth flashed a warm smile. He pushed the pad of paper toward her and handed over the pen. "I need you to write up your statement. When you're finished, you can change into dry clothes, and I'll drive you and Jake home."

She picked up the pen and began to write. But it

occurred to her that she didn't really want to stay much longer at the B&B.

No way to bail out on the wedding, she couldn't do that to Jazz and Jemma, but maybe once the weekend was over she'd explain to Jemma that it was time for her to go home.

To her family.

JAKE TOLD his story so many times he was growing annoyed. He wanted to see Bree, to make sure she was okay. Deputy Hastings was nice enough, but after grilling him over and over, he then told Jake to write everything down.

Why not just record the conversation?

When Garth brought in a pair of dry clothes, he eyed them suspiciously. "Those aren't mine." He knew full well his duffel was still on the boat.

"They're Dalton's." Garth grinned. "Unless you want to try a uniform? You'd look good as a deputy."

"Ha, ha." He picked up the athletic shorts and T-shirt. "These will be fine."

"I'll take you and Bree back to the B and B." Garth's smile faded. "Jemma and Jazz are worried sick about you both."

"I know." He didn't want to admit how close of a call it had been. Jumping overboard had seemed like a good option at the time, but maybe he should have jumped George to grab the gun away from him instead. "Is George in jail?"

"Yep. And that's where he'll stay."

"Good." Jake relaxed in what felt like the first time since he'd been back in McNally Bay. "I hope he admits to vandalizing the boat, the hit-and-run as well as stabbing Bree's purse."

"Actually, he claims Abe did the hit-and-run." Garth shrugged. "Could be Abe was just trying to scare you off."

"Maybe." A wave of exhaustion hit hard, and he rubbed a hand over his jaw. "Man, I'm too old for this."

"Get dressed and we'll head home." Garth left him alone in the interview room. The dry clothing felt good, and he was anxious to see Bree.

He found her standing next to Garth. He longed to take her into his arms but thought it would be best to wait until they were alone. "I'm ready. Let's get out of here."

As they left the building, Jake stopped short when he caught sight of an older man leaning heavily on his cane. Leon Tate. He suppressed a sigh.

"Thanks for coming, Mr. Tate." Garth's greeting indicated he'd actually invited the old man here. "I wanted to tell you in person that we've arrested the man who killed Lucy."

Leon's gaze darted to Jake, then back to Garth. "Says who?"

"Says the man who confessed to the crime. George Amos was the fourth man on the boat that night. George was in love with Lucy and apparently didn't appreciate being tossed aside for Justin McNally."

"George?" Leon looked confused. "Are you telling me George admitted to killing my little sister?"

"According to the statements of Jake McNally and Brianna Murphy, he did." Garth turned toward him. "Isn't that right, Jake?"

"Yes. George admitted he lost his temper, hit Lucy, causing her to fall overboard." Jake waited a moment, then added, "He also admitted to killing Samuel Delrosa twelve years ago. Apparently, Samuel wanted him to turn himself in, but he refused."

"George Amos." Leon's face tightened. "He claimed Justin did it. He said he was there, saw Justin hit Lucy, sending her overboard."

Jake assumed as much, why else would the old man have carried a grudge against the McNallys over all these years? "I'm sorry, Mr. Tate. But George admitted it to me, and Bree heard him. I was also there the night he hit Sam and threw him down the stairs."

"You were?" Leon's gaze still held suspicion.

He couldn't blame the old man, it couldn't be easy to let go of a falsehood that had been clung to for fifty years. "Yes, I was. And Abe Crowley knew it, he saw me that night. The truth will come out now, Mr. Tate. And I'm truly sorry you had to wait this long to hear it."

Leon's shoulders slumped, and the guy aged ten years in that moment. "I—thanks. For telling me." He slowly turned and made his way back toward his car.

Jake watched him go, feeling bad for him.

The mystery surrounding Lucy Tate's death had finally been solved. He only hoped Leon Tate would finally get a sense of peace from knowing the truth.

Bree was unusually quiet on the ride back to the B&B. Having a near-death experience was enough to make anyone reflect on their life and the choices they'd made.

At least, it had for him. He loved Bree. He wanted to spend the rest of his life with her.

Yet he knew it would be an uphill battle to convince her. Sitting in the back of Garth's squad wasn't the time or the place.

But the minute he had a moment alone, he would tell her.

"Bree! Jake!" Jemma rushed out of the house the moment Garth drove up. "We were so scared! Thank goodness the Coast Guard got there in time!"

"Wait, what? You sent the Coast Guard?"

"Technically, Jazz did. She saw the boat on the water from her bathroom window and knew something was wrong. She saw three people on the boat, instead of two. She immediately called Garth, who contacted the Coast Guard. They were already heading toward you when you and Bree jumped overboard."

"Not exactly the smartest move," Garth said dryly.

"Hey, how was I to know the Coasties were on their way? George had a gun. I wasn't about to stand there and let him shoot us."

"Do you mind if we sit down?" Bree's voice was full of exhaustion.

"Of course not, come inside." Jemma opened the door wide. "It's okay, the wedding rehearsal is finished, and the guests have retired to their rooms."

"Going to bed sounds like a grand idea." Bree's voice held a note of longing.

"Maybe you should go lie down, Bree." Jemma looked concerned. "I can do most of the breakfast tomorrow. My wrist is much better, and you have everything prepped."

"I think I will lie down." Bree avoided Jake's gaze. "Good night."

"Wait, I need to talk to you for a moment." Jake hoped his panic wasn't too noticeable. "Won't take but a second."

"Maybe tomorrow." The way Bree avoided his gaze bothered him. "I'm about to fall on my face. Good night."

Before he could say anything more, Bree slipped through the dining room and disappeared into the master suite. He stared at the closed door, then reluctantly turned away.

No way would Bree leave his sister in the lurch in the midst of a wedding. There would be plenty of time to talk to her in the morning.

In the meantime, he needed to come up with how he'd convince her his feelings were here to stay.

And that he finally understood that his home was with Bree.

BREE HAD a bad feeling Jake wanted to talk to her about his feelings. But it was too late.

She'd made up her mind to leave McNally Bay. Not because she'd almost been stabbed and drowned in the lake, but because the Murphy Equestrian Farm was her home.

And she desperately wanted to see her dad and Quinn.

She fell asleep the moment her head hit the pillow and felt better when she awoke early the following morning. After a quick shower, she headed into the kitchen, not surprised to see Jemma was already there.

"I've started the coffee and set the tables." Jemma gently wiggled her left wrist.

"You took the brace off? Sure that's smart?" Bree helped herself to a cup of tea.

"I'm much better, and I was worried you might not be up to doing the work this morning."

Bree winced at the flash of guilt. "Sorry about that, but I'm here. I'll make the muffins and the bread."

"I'll crack the eggs for the French toast." Jemma pulled a

carton of eggs from the fridge. "I'm sorry you had such a tough time yesterday."

"It's nothing, we're grand now, aren't we?" Bree didn't really want to talk about the events of the day before. As they began fixing the meal, Jazz joined them.

"Guests are starting to arrive." Jazz lifted the coffeepot. "Ready or not, here we go."

For the next two hours, she and Jemma worked side by side in the kitchen making breakfast for six couples.

When Garth came in with Trey, Jemma shooed them out. "Take Dalton, Jake, and Trey to Daisy's."

"Okay." Garth picked Trey up and disappeared as quickly as he'd come.

The full Irish and French toast breakfasts were well received according to Jazz. "They're raving about you."

She and Jemma exchanged a smile. When they finally fed the last guest and had eaten something for themselves, they collapsed at the table.

"One down, one more to go." Jemma sighed and massaged her wrist. She was likely paying for taking the brace off now.

"I'm leaving on after breakfast tomorrow." Bree didn't mean to sound so blunt, but Jemma's reaction was as if she'd lit a firecracker beneath the table.

"But—I need you."

"Not as much as I do." Jake's deep voice came from behind her. He came over and gently tugged her hand, pulling her to her feet. "Let's talk, please?"

She nodded, knowing she couldn't put him off forever. He led the way through the dining room and out to the gazebo. It was already decorated with white tulle and blue flowers for the wedding scheduled later that afternoon.

"We shouldn't be here," she protested, but Jake ignored her.

He clasped both of her hands in his. "Brianna Margaret Murphy, I love you. I know that I've done nothing but hurt you over the past few months, and I'm sorry. I guess I didn't realize how much I was running from the memories of the past."

Oh, how she longed to believe him. It was the first time he'd said the L-word, but she still felt as if they'd been down this road before.

"Jake, I care about you. More than I've cared about any man. But we're too different, aren't we? You're looking for the next adventure and I—well, I just want to go home. I miss my dad, my brother—" Her voice broke, and her eyes dampened. "I miss Ireland."

"Oh, Bree. I miss Ireland, too." Jake tugged her closer, but she tried to resist. Heaven knew she'd go mad if he kissed her again. "Don't you see? I'm not running from the haunting memories anymore. I love you, Bree. From the moment I arrived in Ireland, I knew that it was exactly where I wanted to be."

"Don't be daft! Always planned to move on, you did." Her words were tart, yet she could feel her resolve melting beneath the heat of his gaze.

"It was a knee-jerk reaction to run away. But not anymore. I love you, Bree. I know it will take time to prove it to you, but I'm willing to do whatever it takes to show you how much I care."

She stared at him, trying to read his gaze. But he didn't retreat.

"I love you," he repeated. Then he tugged her closer and wrapped his arms around her. "I love you, and I promise to never leave you. When you almost died in the lake, I realized just how much I couldn't live without you. I don't care about Florence or any other investments. I'm ready to put down roots, with you, Bree. Please give me a chance to prove it."

She couldn't find the words to send him away. Instead, she allowed him to sweep her into his embrace, kissing her with a hunger she recognized deep within herself.

No man had kissed her the way Jake did.

And she knew no man ever would.

"Yes," she whispered when he lifted his head. "I'll give you that chance, because I love you, too, Jake."

She felt the impact of his smile all the way down to her toes.

"Well then, let's head home to Ireland. I still have just over three weeks left on my visa, don't I?"

A grin quirked the corner of her mouth. "Right."

"Great. I need to make the most of it." He kissed her again, showing her without words how he felt.

And she truly believed that this time, Jake would keep his promise.

EPILOGUE

A *week later...*

The rolling green hills visible through a fine mist of rain were a balm to her soul, displaying the forty shades of green Ireland was known for. Beneath the clouds, the first rays of sun peeked over the horizon. She and Jake were headed northwest from the Dublin airport toward her home in Collinstown. It was barely six in the morning, and they'd flown all night, yet she didn't feel the least bit tired.

The past week had passed by quickly. Jake and Oliver had installed the new boat seating. Jake then sold the boat to Oliver Pandal for far less than what he'd originally wanted. Then he'd shocked her by donating the proceeds, all five thousand quid, to Trina's K-9 program.

Jemma's wrist was well enough that she no longer needed the brace. The MRI had shown no tendon damage, which meant no surgery. Bree had helped prepare for the next weekend wedding, making sure Jemma could handle things on her own. Bree felt a twinge of guilt at leaving earlier than planned, but she couldn't ignore the lure of coming home.

Home. Her heart swelled with joy, and she glanced at Jake, who'd insisted on driving. "Beautiful, isn't it?"

"Very." He glanced at her. "At least it will be if your dad doesn't try to string me up by my boxers."

She laughed. "No worries, he'll be more subtle than that."

"That's what I'm afraid of."

She knew he was only joking. Jake was worried about what her father would think of their relationship, but she knew her dad appreciated everything Jake had done in terms of turning their farm around.

The forty-five-minute trip wasn't too bad, and she told Jake to stop for breakfast before heading home. "I don't want to cook when I get there, and you'll enjoy our rashers, won't you?"

"Absolutely." Jake expertly parked her car, the one she'd left at the airport when she'd made the impulsive trip to the US more than two weeks ago.

Her life had changed dramatically since then.

When they finally pulled into the gravel driveway of the Murphy Farm, the rain had stopped and the sun was out. Dark Rogue pranced around his paddock, tossing his regal, beautiful dark head over the white wooden fence.

"Dad!" Bree saw her father and quickly pushed out of the car, running over to greet him. Despite his fifty-nine years, her father was still strong and swept her into his arms for a big hug.

"There's my girl, missed you, I did." Seamus Murphy always smelled like tobacco mixed with peppermint from the candy he adored. "See you brought company."

"You remember Jake." She stepped out of her father's arms and gestured for Jake to come join them.

"I'm not daft, girlie. Of course, I remember the American."

"It's good to see you again, sir." Jake shook his father's hand. "How is Rogue doing?"

"Won another race last weekend." The older man beamed. "Tonight's the last race of the season, I'm hoping he'll make a good showing."

"He will." Jake sounded confident. "Do you have a minute, sir? I have something to ask you."

Her father eyed him thoughtfully for a moment. "I have time. Bree, would you like to head inside to make tea?"

"No, I would not." She wasn't about to leave her father and Jake alone. "Listen, Jake, we can talk to my dad later."

But Jake didn't move, his gaze centered on her father. "Sir, I'd like to ask for your permission to marry your daughter."

Marry? Her? Bree's jaw dropped. Had he gone mad?

"Thought so." Her father nodded. "Planning to drag her back to the states, are you?"

"No, sir. Bree loves Ireland. I'd never take her away from her home."

Her heart swelled with love. "Does Bree have anything to say about it?"

Now Jake looked worried. "What do you mean? I thought you loved it here. You told me Ireland would always be your home."

"Not that, the marriage part. I get a vote on whether or not to marry you, don't I?"

Jake nodded slowly, then reached into his pocket and pulled out a velvet box. "This is a Claddagh ring. I picked it out last week, but if you'd prefer a diamond, I'm happy to trade up to something flashier."

She caught her breath, the gold Claddagh ring, the traditional Irish ring with two hands holding a heart, was perfect. "Oh, Jake. I love it. What would I do with a stupid diamond?"

He smiled in relief. "Brianna Margaret Murphy, will you please marry me?"

She smiled through her tears of happiness and threw herself into his arms. "Yes, Jake Justin McNally. I will marry you, as long as your entire family will come to Ireland to celebrate with us."

He hugged her close. "I think we can manage that."

Her father cleared his throat. "I guess I'll be giving you my blessing. Just don't ever hurt her, understand?"

"I promise I won't," Jake whispered.

If you enjoyed the McNallys why not try my Lifeline Air Rescue Series? A Doctor's Promise

DEAR READER

I hope you enjoyed this conclusion of my McNally Family series! I had so much fun writing about these siblings and the beautiful area surrounding Lake Michigan and the glimpse into life in fabulous Ireland.

Reviews are crucial for authors, so if you would be so kind as to leave a review on the retailer from where you purchased this book, I would be so grateful!

Also, please take a moment to visit my website at www.laurascottbooks.com. I offer an exclusive free Crystal Lake novella for all newsletter subscribers. This novella is not available for sale on any retail site. You can find me on Twitter https://twitter.com/laurascottbooks or Facebook https://www.facebook.com/LauraScottBooks/.

Lastly, I've included the first chapter of my Crystal Lake Series, *A Soldier's Promise* here.

Until next time,
Laura Scott

9 781949 144055